T0038189

IS MOTHER DEAD

IS MOTHER DEAD

A novel
by
Vigdis Hjorth

Translated by Charlotte Barslund

VERSO
London • New York

NORLA
NORWEGIAN LITERATURE ABROAD

This translation has been published with the financial support of NORLA

This paperback edition first published by Verso 2023
This English-language edition published by Verso 2022, 2023
Originally published as *Er Mor Død*
© Cappelen Damm 2020
Translation © Charlotte Barslund 2022, 2023

1 3 5 7 9 10 8 6 4 2

Verso
UK: 6 Meard Street, London W1F 0EG
US: 388 Atlantic Avenue, Brooklyn, NY 11217
versobooks.com

Verso is the imprint of New Left Books

ISBN-13: 978-1-80429-184-9
ISBN-13: 978-1-83976-433-2 (US EBK)
ISBN-13: 978-1-83976-432-5 (UK EBK)

British Library Cataloguing in Publication Data
A catalogue record for this book is available from the British Library

The Library of Congress Has Cataloged the Hardback Edition as Follows:

Names: Hjorth, Vigdis, author. | Barslund, Charlotte, translator.
Title: Is mother dead : a novel / by Vigdis Hjorth ; translated from the
    Norwegian by Charlotte Barslund.
Other titles: Er mor død. English
Description: London ; New York : Verso, 2022. | 'Originally published as Er
    mor død'
Identifiers: LCCN 2022007207 (print) | LCCN 2022007208 (ebook) | ISBN
    9781839764318 (hardcover) | ISBN 9781839764332 (US ebook) | ISBN
    9781839764325 (UK ebook)
Subjects: LCSH: Mothers and daughters – Fiction. | LCGFT: Thrillers
    (Fiction). | Novels.
Classification: LCC PT8951.18.J58 E713 2022 (print) | LCC PT8951.18.J58
    (ebook) | DDC 839.823/74 – dc23/eng/20220311
LC record available at https://lccn.loc.gov/2022007207
LC ebook record available at https://lccn.loc.gov/2022007208

Typeset in Electra by Biblichor Ltd, Scotland
Printed and bound by CPI Group (UK) Ltd, Croydon, CR0 4YY

Is Mother Dead

A NOVEL

Vigdis Hjorth

She would contact me if Mum died. She has to, hasn't she?

I called Mum one evening. It was in the spring, I know that because the next day I went for a walk round Borøya with Pax, and it was warm enough for us to sit on the bench by Osesund and eat our sandwiches. I had barely slept that night because of the phone call and I was glad to be seeing someone that morning and that that someone was Pax, I was still shaking. I was ashamed to have called Mum. It was against the rules and yet I'd done it. I'd promised myself I wouldn't, and they wouldn't want me to anyway. Nor did she pick up the phone. The busy signal started the moment she declined the call. And yet I called her back. Why? I don't know. What was I hoping for? I don't know. And why this paralysing shame?

Luckily I was going for a walk with Pax round Borøya the next day, I could hardly wait, my inner trembling would lessen once I had talked to Pax. I picked him up from the station and the moment he got into the car I told him what I had done, called Mum, I offloaded on Pax all the way to the car park, all the way round Borøya, but he didn't think it was strange that I had called Mum. *I don't think it's strange that you want to talk to your Mum.* I still felt ashamed, but less shaky. But I've nothing to say to her, I said. I don't know what I would have said if she had picked up the phone, I said. Perhaps I had hoped that something would spring to mind if she answered her phone and said, Hello? In her own voice.

The situation was of my own making. I had chosen to leave my marriage, my family and my country almost three decades before, although it hadn't felt as if I'd had a choice. I had left my marriage and my family for a man they regarded as suspect and a vocation they regarded as offensive, exhibiting paintings they found humiliating, I didn't come home when Dad fell ill, when Dad died, when he was buried, what were they to make of that? They thought it was awful, that I was awful, for them what was awful was that I left, humiliated them, failed to turn up for Dad's funeral, but for me things had gone wrong long before that. They didn't understand or they refused to understand, we didn't understand one another and yet I had called Mum. I had called Mum as if it was an OK thing to do. No wonder she hadn't picked up. What was I thinking? What had I expected? That she would pick up the phone as if it was an OK thing to do? Who did I think I was, did I think I mattered in any way, that she would be pleased? Real life isn't like the Bible where the return of the prodigal son is celebrated with a feast. I was ashamed to have broken my vow and to have revealed to Mum and Ruth, whom Mum would definitely have told about the call, that I was unable to stick to it, while they, my Mum and my sister, kept their vow and wouldn't dream of calling me. They must have heard that I was back in the country. They probably googled me regularly, they had found out that a retrospective of my work would be taking place, that I had a Norwegian mobile number now, otherwise Mum would

2

have answered the phone. They were strong and steadfast while I was weak, childish, and I felt and acted like a child. Besides, they didn't *feel* like talking to me. But did I *feel* like talking to Mum? No! But then again I was the one who had called! I was ashamed that something in me *wanted* to talk to her and that by calling I showed her that something in me *wanted* to, did I need something from her? What would that be? Forgiveness? Perhaps that was what she told herself. But I hadn't had a choice! But then why did I call, what did I *want*? I don't know! Mum and Ruth thought I called because I'd repented, they hoped I had repented and was hurting, that I missed them and wanted to make amends, but Mum didn't pick up the phone because it wasn't going to be so easy that the moment I was back in Norway and wanted to get in touch with them, they were ready to welcome me with open arms, oh no. I was to fully experience my choice and repent it. But I didn't repent! To them it looked as if I had made a choice, and that irritated me, but irritation is easy to bear, irritation is nothing compared to shame, why this paralysing shame? Talking to Pax helped. We walked on the shale paths along the sea where ducks and swans were swimming, and in the bend by Osesund I picked a colts-foot, I told myself it meant good luck. Once I got back I put it in water in an eggcup, but it soon wilted. Now it's autumn, September 1. My first Norwegian autumn in thirty years.

I had been drinking when I called, not a lot, a few glasses of wine, but I had been drinking or I wouldn't have called. I found her number on www.1881.no and entered it with trembling fingers. Had I thought rationally, I wouldn't have called. If prior to that, I had made myself think clearly, imagine the most likely scenarios should Mum answer her phone, I wouldn't have called, I would have understood it wouldn't lead to anything other than distress for both of us. It was an unrealistic, irrational phone call. Nor did she pick up. My mum and my sister were rational human beings, I was irrational, was that why I felt shame? If I had been a rational human being, I would have realised that if Mum had answered her phone, it wouldn't have led to anything that could be called a conversation anyway. A conversation between Mum and me had become impossible. But that didn't curb my irrational impulse, I didn't want to think clearly, I wanted to follow this sudden and for me surprisingly strong impulse, what depths did it come from? That's what I'm trying to find out.

4

I hadn't had anything that could be called a conversation with Mum for thirty years, perhaps I never had. I met Mark, applied in secret to the institute in Utah where he taught and was accepted, I travelled with him across the sea, away from my marriage, my family, it all happened during one hot summer. It's true, as they say, that one look is all it takes, one glance, and I burned with an inextinguishable flame; it was seen as betrayal and a slap in the face. I wrote them a long letter at the time to explain why I had done what I had done, I poured out my heart in that letter, but the short reply I received was as if I hadn't written to them in the first place. A short, blunt reply with threats of ostracism, but stating that if I 'came to my senses' and returned home immediately, I might be forgiven. They wrote as if I were a child and they my guardians. They reeled off what it had cost them financially and emotionally to bring me up, I owed them quite a lot. They meant, I understood, that I was literally indebted to them. They seriously believed that I would give up my love and my work because they had paid for tennis lessons when I was a teenager. They didn't take me seriously, they didn't try to understand me, instead they made threats. Perhaps their own parents had had such power over them once, perhaps they had themselves trembled so on encountering their parents' words, especially the written ones, that they thought their own would have just as strong an impact on me.

I wrote another long letter explaining what the art course meant to me and who Mark was, again they replied as if I hadn't written, as if they hadn't read my letter, they reiterated how much money they had spent buying me a flat so I could live near the university while I studied Law, and paying for my wedding, of which by my immature behaviour I had now made a mockery for all the world to see, betrayed a newly minted husband, leaving his family humiliated and incredulous. I had to get 'these thoughts which this M' had planted in me out of my head. Only a few chosen individuals ever succeeded in making a living from the arts, and reading between the lines it was clear I wouldn't be one of them. It hurt me as did the notion that they genuinely appeared to believe their words would make me give up my new life, travel home to emotional blackmail and mould myself to fit their expectations, which was something I regarded as an act of self-harm. I didn't reply to that letter, in December I sent them a Christmas card and included a friendly but guarded description of the little town where we lived, our house, the patch of land where we grew tomatoes, the changing of the seasons in Utah. I wrote as if their last letter hadn't been written, I did to them what they had done to me, Merry Christmas! I had a similar card back, short but guarded, Happy New Year! From time to time I would send them an exhibition catalogue or a postcard from a trip, I wrote to them when John was born and sent them a photo. He got a letter back, Dear John, welcome to the world, love Grannie, Granddad and Aunt Ruth. When he turned one, he got a silver cup in the post, best wishes Grannie, when he turned two, a silver spoon, when he turned three, a fork. During the first few years my sister would send me short texts about Mum's or Dad's health if there was any news to report, a kidney stone operation, a slip on the ice, there was no salutation, no questions, just a line about my parents' physical condition, Ruth. As they were in fairly good health, these messages were rare. The implication was that she was to be pitied for having to take care of them singlehandedly, that I was selfish, having gone off seemingly without caring. I believed she only wrote them to make me feel bad, but perhaps I took it that way because something inside me did feel bad? I replied: Get well soon. But after the triptychs *Child and Mother 1* and *Child and Mother 2* were exhibited in Oslo, my city, in one of its most prestigious galleries, well attended and with extensive media coverage, Ruth's occasional messages and Mum's seasonal greetings ceased. In a roundabout way, through Mina, whose mum still lived nearby, I learned that they found my paintings distressing, that I brought shame on my family, on Mum especially. John continued to get birthday cards, but the words were less warm, apart from that there was silence. I knew nothing about my parents' daily life. I assumed that it was routine, as it is for most old and comfortably-off people, that they still lived in the house they had moved to when I was a teenager, in a smarter part of the city than the house which belonged to my childhood, I hadn't heard anything to the contrary. I would have known if they had downsized and decided to give Ruth and me an advance on our inheritance, they were honest people when it came to money. It would have been easy to imagine them in the rooms in the house where I myself had lived, but I didn't. Fourteen years ago I was working in a borrowed studio in SoHo, New York, Mark was at the Presbyterian Hospital, when I had a message from Ruth telling me that Dad had had a stroke and was in hospital, that was all it said, she didn't ask me to come. During the next three weeks she wrote several short messages about Dad's condition, using partly inexplicable medical terminology, there was nothing inviting in the words, no salutation, not my name, just short bulletins she felt obliged to send, I never thought she wanted me to come. My presence would seem intrusive. I had no part to play, it would only make things awkward for everyone, I felt awkward just thinking about it, and I wished Dad a speedy recovery. On November 20 she wrote that he had died, which surprised me, at that moment I was still in the studio in SoHo, Mark was still at the Presbyterian, I didn't go, I didn't even think of travelling back or of going to the funeral. Nor did they ask me, Ruth wrote that he would be buried at such-and-such time and place, and that was it. The day after the funeral I got a message sent from her phone, but it was from both of them, it said *we*, it was signed *Mum and Ruth*, a goodbye message. Mum had taken it very hard that I hadn't come back to Dad's sickbed, to Dad's funeral, it had nearly killed her, it said, and in a way I had killed her symbolically, that was how they phrased it, as far as I recall, I didn't save the message, I deleted it immediately. I regret that now, it would have been interesting to relive the moment, I mean, to read it today, now, in September. I saw it as an excuse to reject me for good and blame the *finality* on me. The birthday letters to John ceased.

We were no longer 'not on speaking terms', but actual enemies, I realised, it didn't bother me, I worked, I looked after Mark, after John. The house was sold, Mum bought a flat, I received a set of accounts, my inheritance from Dad and a formal letter from a solicitor, no mention of Mum's new address, but so what. When we happened to make a brief visit to Norway we never told them, when Mark died I didn't tell them, they had never met him and had never expressed any wish to meet him. When

John moved to Europe, to Copenhagen, four years ago, I didn't tell them, why should I, they had never met him. I talked to Mina, I talked to Pax. But when Skogum Art Museum decided to put on a major retrospective of my work in two years' time, the city of my childhood started haunting me in my dreams. As my conversations with the curator about which works to include became more frequent, it also started to haunt me when I was awake. I had promised to contribute at least one new work, but I was unable to produce anything, I stood in front of various canvases for days, but my heart wasn't in it. On further reflection I realised that I hadn't painted anything significant since the manic rapture that followed Mark's death, the years I spent in the studio, processing my grief at losing him. Now it had eased, was that why, and because I was now living alone in everything that was once ours? I decided to move back home, I still called Norway home, initially just for a while, until the opening of the exhibition. I didn't tell them, why should I? I let my house in Utah and with the rental income and my widow's pension from Mark, I was able to rent a modern flat in a new part of Oslo by the fjord with a conservatory which could double up as my studio. Now I live in the same city as Mum, four and a half kilometres from her, I've looked up her new address on 1881, she lives in Arne Bruns gate number 22, closer to the city centre than the houses where I grew up, I also found her phone number on 1881.

I spent the first few months mainly indoors, I didn't recognise the city anymore and felt like a stranger, besides it was late winter. Grey fog drifted across the partly frozen fjord, the ridges on the horizon looked like sleeping Dalmatians, the pavements were covered with compacted snow and ice. On the rare occasions I ventured outside, I would sometimes be conscious of Mum's presence four and a half kilometres away. In contrast to the past thirty years, there was now a real chance that I might bump into her. Then again, she was unlikely to be outdoors in this weather, in this cold, with snow on the icy pavements and risk breaking her hip. Old women are scared of breaking their hips. She had to be well into her eighties by now. I was standing by the ticket machine at the station one February afternoon when an old woman asked me if I could help her buy a ticket. I had just learned how to do it myself and I helped her, she stood close to me and I was touched by how trusting she was, her handbag open, her purse open. Once she got her ticket, she asked me if I could help her up the stairs, I couldn't say no. She grabbed my arm with one hand, the handrail with the other, her handbag hanging around her neck, dangling with every step, she was so slow that I feared I would miss my train, but I couldn't let go, of course. I counted the steps in order to calm myself down, there were twenty-two. On the platform she thanked me profusely, I said it was nothing, she was going to visit her daughter, she said, and I felt embarrassed.

Had I called Mum to get to know her again? To see who she was now? To talk to Mum as if she weren't my mum, but an ordinary human being, a random woman at a railway station? That's impossible. Not because she isn't an ordinary human being with all the associated flaws, but because a mother can never be an ordinary human being to her children, and I am one of her children. Even if she has discovered new interests, learned new skills, changed her personality, she will always be the mother from the past to me. Perhaps she hates that that's how it is, being a mother is a cross to bear. Mum is fed up with being a mum, with being my mum, and in a way she isn't now, but as long as her daughter is alive, she can't be safe. I wonder if Mum always felt that being my mum was incompatible with being herself? What if Mum had wished not to be my mum right from the moment I was born? But there was no escape for her, no matter how hard she tried. Or maybe she succeeded, perhaps she forgot that she was my mum during my long absence, and then I call to remind her of it. To her, it must have seemed to come out of the blue.

She'll say she has changed. It's understandable that parents, once they are older and wiser, want their children to look at them afresh. But no one can expect or demand of the children that they forget the image of their mother as they experienced her in their childhood or that they erase the image of their mother created over the first thirty years of their life and instead see her objectively as a seventy or eighty-year-old.

It's easier for people who see their parents regularly. Most of my friends who see their parents regularly view them more kindly now that their rough edges have been smoothed by life's ups and downs, they have become more indulgent and likeable, and some have acknowledged their mistakes as parents, and even apologized for them. Perhaps Ruth has experienced Mum growing warmer and wiser, that must be good for both Ruth and Mum. Slowly the old image is replaced with a new one, or the image of the young and the old meld and the image produced by this fusion is easier to live with. Someone who is in regular contact with their mother and who talks about the past with her, helps re-create the past, together they make history. That's probably what happens. Ruth probably remembers the past the way Mum wants her to remember it.

But I've also heard stories of how those traits in the mother which were worst for the child during childhood have intensified during her life to the extent that they end up dominating her personality. Mina's mother nagged and picked on Mina day in day out, year in year out, and she still does except now more harshly, more mercilessly. Mina visits her in the nursing home every day with rissoles and soup and is met with accusations and barbs, why does Mina bother? Because if she were to lose her temper and accuse her mother of being unreasonable, her mother would have her beliefs about life in general and Mina in particular confirmed, Mina says, and she is not going to give her the satisfaction. The fact that her mother's words appear to have no effect on Mina, is Mina's way of punishing her mother. Child and mother.

Once I had decided to move back, my work improved, I started a painting that I felt was promising, it came with me across the sea, but when the practicalities relating to my move were completed and I was supposed to go back to work, nothing happened. I started another picture, a spring-like painting, then I called Mum, then my inspiration dried up. I had intended to visit museums and galleries as I usually do when I'm stuck, but became aware of a fear of public spaces I hadn't experienced before. Was it because I had been on my own so much after Mark's death that I had become a recluse, or was it because I no longer knew the city or because Mum lived in it and I feared bumping into her? Once outdoors, I notice all the old women. They board trains all hunched up and slowly. They grip handles, lean against walls and doors, get up laboriously when the train approaches, check the contents of their old-fashioned handbags to make sure everything is there, purse, glasses, keys, I had started doing it myself, where are my glasses? At the chemist they sit on one of the few chairs, with introverted faces, they don't read a newspaper, they don't check their phone, they turn away from the world, or the opposite, they turn to the most immediate part of it, the number on the ticket between their lightly trembling fingers, the display board where new red numbers keep flashing up, everything happens so quickly, anxious that the number might change again before they have had time to get up and walk to the counter to get their vital medication. Old bodies ail. Does Mum's body ail? Why do I want to know that? Does Mum have a hearing aid? Why do I want to know that? I wonder. Information we can't access is especially tantalising. In the absence of information, I invent her. What is it I want to know? I wonder how she is. Not because I care about her, not in that sense, but: How have you experienced it all? How was it for you? And how do you see the situation now, the existential one which we share, what do you think about our situation? Will I never know? Will she ever know what it has been like, what it is like for me? She must wonder about it, surely? About what I think, about how I am, no matter how angry, how resentful she is, she must wonder about it because in spite of everything I am her nearly sixty-year-old child.

How old is Mum now? Many years ago I had a text message from Ruth: Mum is seventy today. I replied: Happy birthday and best wishes. It must have been before Dad died so she must be eighty-five now or older. I don't remember which year she was born or her date of birth, it's not as easy to find out these things as you would think. I could call someone in the family and ask them, Ruth or Mum's brother, he is listed on 1881, but I can't call them and ask when Mum's birthday is, that's a no-no. It's in the autumn. I remember her fiftieth birthday, I think, because Thorleif came to that one, we stood in the garden underneath the fruit trees. Perhaps I'm making it up. But I remember how I struggled to breathe, the knot in my stomach I always had on such occasions when the family showed its public face, the feeling of having had a script thrust at me, the expectation that I would play my part, the loyal daughter of a lawyer, the wife of a lawyer, the law student, I was ill at ease with this role and the fact that the others, Thorleif, Ruth and the other guests were faithful to the script written by Mum and Dad, mostly Dad, and with the feeling of being controlled and how I couldn't be myself, and besides I didn't know who I was and I couldn't find that out where I was, in Mum and Dad's garden, in Mum and Dad's company, I remember it clearly, the feeling of being trapped and a smouldering frustration which I feared at some point I wouldn't be able to

17

suppress, and then what? Thorleif in awe of Dad, Thorleif agreeing with everything Dad said, Thorleif's laughter when Dad mocked my 'artistic pretensions' and rolling his eyes because I wanted to apply to the Arts and Crafts Academy, the arty-farty academy, as he called it, how Thorleif laughed. I had thought from an early age that Dad wasn't my real father. When I first heard the story of Hedvig who turns out not to be Hjalmar Ekdal's biological daughter in *The Wild Duck*, I thought, that's it! Except that I would never shoot myself if it turned out to be true, no, I would feel relieved and free, I think. Mum had been with another man, perhaps just for one night, got pregnant, and Dad suspected that she had been with someone else because I didn't look like him, and every time Mum looked at me, she was reminded of her infidelity, she felt ashamed and lived in fear of being found out, that had to be it, it explained everything. Why she jumped whenever I entered a room unexpectedly. *You scared me!* For the umpteenth time Dad told the joke about two thieves who want to rob a museum, one asks the other how they will know which paintings are the most valuable, the ugliest ones his mate replies, ha-ha. It's not art just because no one understands it, ha-ha. If you haven't become a conservative by the time you've grown up, you haven't got a brain. I was the brainless one. My attempts to counter this argument were met with indulgent smiles, every hint of protest was regarded as an immature wish to oppose for the sake of opposition, to get attention, to be laughed at. Thorleif laughed and my throat tightened, but the anger has burned itself out in me now. Mum's burning gaze when she realised I wasn't going to give a speech and Dad's blue and glacial stare no longer bother me. It has all burned itself out in me now.

They know I'm in town. Mina called me, she had run into Ruth at Langvann, and when she told her that I had moved back for a while, she already knew.

They don't get in touch. They are principled and proud, they made up their minds back when I didn't turn up for Dad's funeral, and that decided the matter.

I called Mum. It was in the evening, it might have been ten o'clock, I expected her to be alone. I imagined that she was watching television. No, it's with hindsight that I imagine it so, at the time I didn't imagine anything specific, I called on impulse, I got the idea into my head and rang her before I had time to have second thoughts. I had had a few glasses of wine. Mum didn't pick up. That's to say, my call rang out. Perhaps Ruth has blocked my number on her phone? Ruth probably thinks it won't do Mum any good to talk to me, and that's probably true in one way. Ruth knows that I'm in town and is afraid that I might call Mum. She wants to prevent any contact. My sister protects Mum and protects herself by blocking my number on her phone. I don't think Mum could do it herself. She has always been useless with technology from what I remember. Though that might have changed, especially since Dad died. Perhaps Mum has grown more adept at practical stuff, but I tell myself that Ruth does most of it, especially when it comes to her phone. But perhaps I only think Ruth has blocked my number because I'm hoping there is something in Mum that *wants* me to call her. Mum isn't indifferent. No matter how much she has managed to remove me from her life, she hasn't managed it to the extent that she is indifferent towards my possible indifference. By calling I bestowed on Mum a kind of significance. I think she wants that. Even if she thinks I was calling to accuse her of something, but she can't still believe that after all these years, thirty years.

In the house next to the one where I grew up lived an old woman, a widow called Mrs Benzen. All the children were scared of Mrs Benzen, she would order us to be quiet when we played, tell us off if we leaned against her fence, threaten us with the police if we picked a single cherry from the branches of her tree that overhung the pavement. I came to realise that Mum, who was a young woman back then, was also afraid of Mrs Benzen. It's one of my earliest memories, and it still pains me to think of it. I might have been seven years old, I was playing on my own, bouncing a ball against the garage door, I threw it too high, the ball landed in Mrs Benzen's garden, and because I couldn't see anyone in her windows, I ran into her garden to retrieve it from the flower bed by the porch, then I ran back and was busy playing with my ball again when I saw Mrs Benzen come out of her front door, head for our garden gate, march through it and toward me, she grabbed my arm and dragged me to our front door, she rang the doorbell, Mum opened. When she saw Mrs Benzen she took a step back and her face went white, Mrs Benzen told Mum off because she hadn't brought up her kid properly, me, who had trespassed on her garden and trodden on her peonies, Mum was silent. I hadn't expected her to defend me and would rather have been told off by her than by Mrs Benzen, but hoped that she would ask me first what had happened, but Mum did none of those things, she stood mute and frightened and childish in her encounter with Mrs Benzen and afterward collapsed on a chair, her legs shaking. Mum's mouth speechless, what had I just witnessed? That she wasn't strong though she seemed mighty to me? At some point she must have changed from fearful and mute to chatty and conversing, when was that?

But perhaps her fear and muteness returned when Dad died, and that explained why she didn't pick up when I called, she is scared of me. Her phone rings and Mum's chest tightens at the thought that it might be me. Mum reflects on her life as the elderly are said to do, an old image of me pops up and her heart starts to pound from fear. Mum sees a newspaper advert for my retrospective and the blood freezes to ice in her veins. Fear makes people inventive, Mum imagines me in my absence, and she makes me out to be worse than I am. But I'm guessing she feels more outraged than frightened. Besides I'm probably overestimating my importance. The fact that Mum didn't pick up when I called doesn't mean that I'm associated with any kind of emotion. Mum just doesn't want to have to deal with me. Mum has probably taught herself methods to avoid any memories that include me. It's understandable given the situation, and yet it's strange to think of. That's how our lives have turned out.

September 4, it's two o'clock in the afternoon. From my studio I can see the sky, it's very blue now, very high. I can also see the fjord, the September sea alternates between steel grey and steel blue, the big ships smell of oil. If I look down from the balcony I can see the mighty maples either side of the street below me, they have only just started to turn yellow. Four and a half kilometres away Mum lives and breathes. Unless she has travelled to warmer parts of the world like many old people do when it gets cold. But it isn't that cold yet, I have the balcony door open, I'm facing the sun, if Mum has a balcony and she probably does, she might have her balcony door open just like me, perhaps she is looking at the same sun as I am, the sun is yellow and warms everyone. The slight sharpness in the air, which tells me it's autumn, is fresh against my face, autumn is a good time, the new school year starts in the autumn, clean sheets of paper and all that. Mum probably won't travel abroad until November. She might be planning her trip right now, this very moment she is sitting with her friend Rigmor at the kitchen table in Arne Bruns gate 22, a place I find difficult to visualise, studying glossy travel brochures and *dreaming* herself away. Mum has long since come to terms with the loss of her daughter. She is going to make the most of her old age. Why can't I come to terms with that? I've come to terms with losing my mum, but I can't come to terms with Mum coming to terms

24

with losing her daughter? Then again this particular thought has barely crossed my mind these past thirty years. Is it because I'm back home that the situation seems strange now? It didn't at the beginning, not in the first few months when I was overwhelmed with practicalities, unpacking, furnishing, attending frequent planning meetings with the curator, slowly rediscovering the city of my birth, it was much changed, much bigger, I liked it, but when that was all over and I was meant to be starting work, when the winter eased off and I was sitting on the balcony looking across the sea at the ferries arriving early in the morning, then I started thinking. Is it because I myself now stand on the threshold of the age of reflection? Because I no longer merely look ahead, but also back? Because I have a grandchild, is it a form of sentimentality, is it this *never again* with which I find it hard to reconcile?

I called Mum, she didn't pick up.

Ruth thinks talking to me won't do Mum any good. Mum can't take any more. Mum hasn't been able to cope with what has already happened, my sudden departure, my work, which *exposed her to shame*, that I didn't come over during the difficult time, for Dad's funeral. Mum is finally over me and any contact with me might reopen old wounds. I understand.

But now that my anger at being ostracised and branded the black sheep of the family has burned itself out in me, perhaps Mum's disappointment in me might have burned itself out too? Ruth won't take the chance. The risk of Mum being beside herself and anxious after a conversation with me is considerable, and Ruth wants to avoid it. It's understandable, she is the one who has to deal with Mum when she gets upset. I imagine that Mum gets upset quite often, but perhaps I want her to be upset, to miss me and to wonder how I am, and so I project that wish onto her. That's probably what's happening here because Mum's ability to shrug off anything unpleasant has always been great, fundamental to her character and it still is, I'm quite sure of this because I might not have been in contact with her for thirty years, but I'd had intimate contact with her in the twenty plus years before that. And those years have marked me, they won't have been reduced to ashes, they can't be dismissed, what I experienced then, especially in my early years, Mum's most private persona before she became good at hiding herself. Although both will have changed during the subsequent thirty years, with the passage of time, you can't expect a child's experience of the mother of its childhood to change as a result of time alone.

Only through regular contact can the childhood image of the mother be changed. My sister has probably changed her childhood image of Mum as a result of time spent together on a regular basis. That's the benefit of regular contact, anything painful is slowly neutralised. But there might be a price to pay. What is it?

I could drive to Arne Bruns gate 22 to see where she lives.
I wouldn't dream of it.

I was in my studio squeezing emerald green paint out of a tube when my journey to school came back to me, when Mum and I still walked it together. It was a sunny day in April, the sky was high and the buds on the tall birches glowed lime green in the cool air, I wore a new knitted jumper, it was green. I would have been happy if it hadn't been for Mum's anxiety. We were going to a parents' evening and Mum was just as scared of the strict Miss Bye as she was of Mrs Benzen, she feared that Miss Bye would be just as exasperated with me as Mrs Benzen was and thus with Mum as my parent, she feared that Miss Bye thought that Mum had failed at her most important task; being a mother. Dad being a lawyer was no use when he wasn't physically here, Mum was defenceless. I sensed it and grew nervous for both of us, Mum's footsteps slowed the closer we got to the school, but then again being late wouldn't be good either. She stopped at the school gates, turned to me and said, You haven't done anything wrong, have you? I didn't think so, but I couldn't be sure. Sometimes I would have bad thoughts about Miss Bye, but no one could know that, could they? I shook my head cautiously and in we went, found the right door and Mum's hand in its cardigan sleeve knocked on it. Miss Bye called out *Enter* and Mum opened the door, Miss Bye was sitting at the teacher's table with two chairs in front where we sat down, and Mum slumped. Miss Bye looked at her papers, Mum looked at her hands, Miss Bye addressed Mum, *Mrs Hauk*, and Mum lifted her head with moist eyes, she must have been in her early thirties at that point. Miss Bye said I could do better in math, Mum nodded and bowed her head. But I was good at reading and spelling, she said, and particularly good at joined-up writing, as Mum continued to look down. Miss Bye produced my exercise book, turned to the letter æ and held it up, and Mum raised her gaze. And take a look at this, Miss Bye said, and turned to the page where I had drawn a border, Mum looked at the exercise book and then briefly at me. Johanna has a talent for drawing, Miss Bye said, and that's why the head teacher would like her to draw the school's Constitution Day invitation, would you like to do that? Miss Bye turned to me with something that looked like genuine pride. Awestruck I nodded. The head teacher will be so pleased, Miss Bye said, got up and held out her hand, Mum took it, curtsied, it was over, the danger had passed. Back in the corridor Mum breathed a sigh of relief, bent down, hugged me and whispered, That's what I've been saying all along.

What had she been saying and to whom? To me she had never said anything about joined-up writing or borders or Constitution Day, but that meant nothing, the walk home was giddy. We went to the patisserie in Dahls Plass and had Napoleon cakes, Mum repeated the bit about my talent and the Constitution Day invitation twice, I was so happy! *That's what I've been saying all along.* I was looking forward to Mum telling Dad, but he didn't come home that night, Dad was in London. That evening just as I was falling asleep, it clicked with me. Mum had told Dad that I had a talent for drawing, but

Dad had disagreed. My heart swelled at the thought that Mum said nice things about me to Dad who didn't believe them, but they were true.

When did she stop, when did she become Dad's completely?

I have no idea if Mum is still of a cheerful disposition, but I suspect so, so fundamental is her readily accepting mind, I think. I expect she has managed to ignore her griefs and losses, an art she mastered fully back when I knew her, unless all I have of her now is merely a dream of the past. I hope that she has kept her cheerful disposition. Mum was fearful, childish, unpredictable and for that reason frightening, but she lacked gravitas. Mum existed in the world with a fundamental lightness. Liking Mum was easy, I believe, for anyone who wasn't her daughter, it was probably easier for other people to be with Mum than it was for me, but she didn't spend much time with other people, the world for mothers wasn't big back when I was a child, there was the house, the garden, the immediate surroundings, the neighbourhood, the shops, but Mum was able to talk in an amusing manner about what had happened in the shops. I had simultaneously admired and been irritated by Mum's lightness, Mum's ability to shrug off anything unpleasant rather than explore it, to focus on something else, a new dress, carpe diem and all that – except she wouldn't have used that expression. That ability must have been an advantage to her, and to Dad, and possibly to me as well. Because what would have happened if Mum had thrown all her energy into exploring uncomfortable and difficult issues, it would have given me a different childhood, possibly a more difficult one. No, I'm not mocking

Mum's lightness, I take it seriously, and I can't believe other than that Mum is still light yet strong. Except Ruth doesn't understand how strong Mum is or she doesn't want to understand it because if Mum is strong, Ruth's strength matters less. Or Mum doesn't show Ruth her strength because Mum feeds on Ruth's care, they convince one another that Mum couldn't cope with being in touch with me.

I imagine Ruth ringing Mum's doorbell and Mum letting her in and making some acerbic but funny comment about Rigmor, which makes Ruth laugh. Perhaps visiting Mum is fun. Nevertheless it's easy to imagine how visiting Mum might be a chore, because although Mum could be light-hearted, she would often feel terribly sorry for herself and she probably still does. On rare occasions, right in the middle of Mum wallowing in self-pity, she would start to laugh at herself, and it was a relief when Mum was able to take herself less seriously. I feel a delicious warmth at the memory. But I tell myself that Mum takes herself very seriously now. Is that because she is old and needs help and she doesn't have the fortitude which taking yourself less seriously requires and because she feels betrayed and humiliated by me? Or perhaps it's the exact opposite, perhaps Mum feels more cheerful than she used to because she doesn't have to deal with me anymore? I don't think so. I think visiting Mum as often as Ruth has to must be a chore, and I'm guessing that Mum wants Ruth to stay for longer than she has time to and would like to, and makes her disappointment clear when Ruth has to go. Because despite Mum's fundamental lightness, or rather because of it, the spontaneity which lightness presupposes, Mum could, back in the days when I knew her, make her disappointment clear for all to see. Mum was often disappointed in people, especially me. Mum was usually disappointed

34

in people she had just been with, she would come home from seeing Rigmor, say, and express exasperation at something she had said, but in a light and amusing manner, people could be so silly. Mum came home after having visited Ruth in her student hall of residence and was disappointed in the people Ruth lived with and Ruth's boyfriend, who always had to show off, what a know-it-all. And yet a disappointed Mum could still be amusing and engaging. Perhaps Ruth looks forward to visiting Mum because it's entertaining to hear how disappointed she is in Rigmor and in me, if I'm the topic of conversation, but I don't think so. Or she dreads visiting Mum because she knows that Mum will be disappointed when she has to go, as she must do at some point, deep down Mum wants Ruth to give up her life with the know-it-all who became Ruth's husband, and still is, according to 1881, and live with her, but Ruth neither can nor would she want to. In spite of everything. Perhaps Ruth's feelings towards Mum are mixed, it wouldn't surprise me, but Ruth can't acknowledge that ambivalence because it's just her and Mum now. Perhaps Ruth visits Mum mostly out of duty, and perhaps I need to consider the possibility that Ruth doesn't visit Mum. That Ruth broke free like I did? No, that's impossible. Ruth never experienced my strong ambivalence towards Mum because Ruth wanted, or so it looked to me, what Mum and Dad wanted for her, Ruth wasn't rebellious, she didn't leave, she was there when Dad was ill, at Dad's funeral, she supported Mum in her grief. But that doesn't mean Ruth might not have her own reasons to keep her distance, what do I know about what might have happened between them since Dad died, or sooner? But if my sister ever had a wish to free herself from Mum, the fact that I had already left the family would make it harder for her. Mum would be all alone. So instead Ruth has chosen, consciously or subconsciously, to condemn me and my freedom, to agree with Mum that I am a traitor, to take Mum's side, ally herself with Mum, she didn't have a choice.

Ruth hasn't cut contact with Mum, I conclude, Mum and Ruth have one another and they are close, I conclude, because if Ruth had cut contact with Mum, Mum would have picked up the phone when I called.

I know nothing about Mum's daily life. I know her address, but I can't visualise her in the rooms where she lives now. Before Dad died, I could visualise Mum and Dad in the rooms where they lived because I, too, had lived in that house, and after Dad bought me a flat near the university, I would visit my parents regularly as students tend to do. I would come over for Sunday lunch and celebrate Christmas in that house, where else would I go? And after I started seeing Thorleif, I was often in their house because Thorleif and Dad got on well, and Thorleif would ask Dad's advice about legal matters. Visualising Mum and Dad there had been easy, but I hadn't, I had never deliberately conjured up images of them in front of the telly in the TV room or in the hammock on the terrace. But *if* thoughts of Mum and Dad ever crossed my mind, the rooms would, too, as context. Now it's harder to visualise Mum. And now I often try. It must be because I'm once more living in the city of my childhood. When I look up her address on 1881, I see a picture of a large apartment block from the start of the last century. That's all I know. Mum's view from her windows. She lives alone now. I think. I can't be sure. Mum might have got a new boyfriend, older people sometimes do, but I don't think Mum has a new boyfriend. Why not? She's not the type. And what type is that? But more importantly because if Mum had got a new boyfriend, I wouldn't have mattered enough that she had to be so consistent when it came to me, and *not* answer her phone. Mum's and Ruth's principles, their *harshness* towards me, is something they want to *show* me, so what I think and feel must mean something to them. Or maybe I'm exaggerating my importance, perhaps it's merely indifference that makes Mum not answer the phone when I ring – I've rung a few times now. If she genuinely didn't care, she would answer it, if only out of curiosity. Mum's steadfastness must be the product of grim determination or possibly the pure hatred you can feel only towards someone who matters to you, who troubles your mind. I don't think Mum has a new boyfriend, Ruth and Ruth's family are the most important people to Mum now. Ruth has four children, Mina has told me. Ruth has never written a single word about her children to me, the few short texts Ruth sent were about Mum and Dad and were, I assume, written at their request. In time Ruth and Ruth's family have taken up more and more room in Mum's life, my absence increasingly less, and that's good for all concerned. I imagine that the world in general doesn't interest Mum much. It didn't back when I knew her, though much may have happened since, but no, Mum belongs to her own small world, and don't we all.

What does Mum look like? Thirty years older than the last time I saw her, when was it? The spring of 1990, Easter in Rondane National Park? Probably, but I can't recall her image, perhaps I had left mentally even then. Ruth and Reidar had married the year before, I remember what I wore to the wedding, the church, where the wedding reception was held, but I can't recall what Mum or Dad looked like. I remember her perfume, unchanged for all those years, I've considered going to a perfume counter to smell it, but I can't recall the name or the bottle. I remember how she walked, with urgency, her figure and her hands with the rings, unchanged all the years I knew her. Ruth can visualise Mum as she looks now whenever she wants to, Ruth knows if Mum still wears the big yellow gold ring with the red gem on her right hand, Mum has disappeared for me, Mum has become a foreign country, she belongs to a mythical age; unlike Ruth I can't imagine her with a body that has an expiry date.

If I were to learn that Mum was dead or terminally ill, how would I react? If my sister called and said, Mum is dead. Or: Mum is dying. But she wouldn't call, she doesn't have a voice in which she can talk to me. She has made up her mind never to speak to me, and she is the type to stick to her resolutions. If she were to have information which *had* to be shared with me, she would get someone else to make the call, a lawyer, a family *spokesperson*. I wonder how Mum would react if she were told she was terminally ill, she was always so focused on the world outside herself. What images and memories would haunt her? Mum under a duvet knowing the end is nigh, that soon it will grow dark, rage, rage against the dying of the light, I can easily imagine her raging, protesting, not yet full of years, do not go gentle into that good night, and I imagine that her unique life force would become visible right at that moment, that it would surge at the very point of its extinction. I imagine her death in order to beat her to it because I won't get to be a part of it, because she doesn't want me there. I won't be summoned, and if someone were to suggest that I should be, she would refuse and rage, rage against it, as far as she is concerned I belong in the past, I'm something unpleasant which has been overcome and dealt with. And were she to be haunted by memories of me and want to see me, she wouldn't say so, for Ruth's sake. And if Mum against my expectation proved strong enough to express such a wish in spite of Ruth, Ruth would do everything in her power to make sure it wasn't honoured, because she doesn't trust me. Our past difficulties would make the situation unpredictable and it could end horribly. My presence might upset Mum, and Ruth can't let Mum die upset, no one would wish that on a dying person.

They are both so far away that I can't visualise them, instead I insert a couple of ghosts in the places where I imagine them to be, it's creepy.

What if I were to go to Arne Bruns gate 22 and ring her doorbell?

The thought terrifies me.

We have become each other's Mrs Benzen.

The other day when I had my hair cut, I was seated next to an old woman who chatted loudly with the hairdresser who was putting her hair in rollers. I was reminded of Mum when she came back from the hairdresser's, walking down Trasoppveien with her long, copper-red hair put up, it was a Saturday, and they were hosting a dinner party, Dad's business associates and their wives, Mum was remarkably pretty, pale and unapproachable with tiny freckles on her nose like the cinnamon dusting on a cappuccino. The old woman next to me might have been pale once, but now her skin was coarse and liver-spotted, her hair thin, there was barely enough to wrap around the rollers, I hoped that Mum's skin, Mum's hair weren't like hers. She was complaining about the leaves falling from the trees and making the pavement slippery, she was frightened of slipping and breaking her hip. Breaking your hip is the beginning of the end, she said, many deaths start with a broken hip. Most people want to live for as long as possible. Had Mum broken her hip? She was born in Fredrikstad, the old woman said. Her father had been a blacksmith at Fredrikstad Shipyard and Engineering, it was back when the smoke from the factories would lie so low on cold winter days that they couldn't see the house next door. The simple mobile phone on the table in front of her rang and she looked at the screen with apprehension, then picked it up as if there were someone in authority on the other end. Yes, she said, she had remembered it. I have remembered it, she said another three times, more slowly now while her face suggested she was beginning to doubt if she had indeed remembered it. She put down her phone with an anxious expression and said it was her daughter. Aren't you lucky to have a daughter who cares about you, the hairdresser said. Perhaps I am, the old woman said, and they both fell quiet. In Fredrikstad, she said, and the hairdresser listened attentively, it's all part of their training. In Fredrikstad when I was a child, the factory whistle would sound in the morning and the workers would hurry to the gates and the women would make packed lunches for their husbands and children, there were seven of them at home. Seven children and her mother had made sure that they all had clean clothes and good packed lunches though her father hadn't made much money working as a blacksmith. Her mother was good at making packed lunches and there would often be surprises, she said, delighted to be telling the story to someone who hadn't heard it before, who might be interested in her childhood in Fredrikstad, a story which I gathered her daughter no longer listened to, she had heard about the packed lunches often enough, sometimes it might be a sugar lump, this was before people knew sugar was bad for the teeth. Her mother had been a remarkable woman, she said. I wondered if Mum had started to speak in this manner so typical of old people, sentences formed a long time ago and now merely repeated. It would certainly represent a big change from how I remembered Mum speaking. Mum's speech had always been slightly hectic and agitated, as if she was nervous, as if she was tormented. Light-hearted on the surface, troubled deep down? But perhaps Mum now speaks as many old people do, slowly, stuttering and apologetically

45

shamefaced at her slowness, it hurts to think about it, I pity old people.

Does Mum go to the hairdresser? Yes. Mum always cared about her appearance, that hasn't changed, it would be sad if Mum had become slovenly and unkempt, but my sister makes sure that doesn't happen. If Mum doesn't make the appointment herself, Ruth will make it for her. I can't imagine Mum so slow in body and speech as the old woman next to me, but something happens to even the sprightliest of people when they reach eighty-five, Mina has told me, she works with the elderly. I think Mum turns eighty-five one of these days, today perhaps? I'm guessing Mum goes to the same hairdresser every time, books her regular appointment, old people don't like change, I, too, visit the same hairdresser every time, but it's a new relationship because I'm new in town. I haven't told my hairdresser that I haven't seen my mum for thirty years although she lives in the same city. You don't share things like that. You can't explain something like that quickly. What does Mum talk to her hairdresser about? Her childhood in Hamar? She doesn't talk about me. It's as if I don't exist. What does Mum say if she is asked about children and grandchildren, the kind of thing hairdressers will usually ask elderly customers, it's all part of their training. But I'm guessing they are also taught that family can be a sore point, that it might lead to much sadness and complication and awkwardness, so tread carefully. Going to have your hair cut should be a pleasant experience, the client also pays for an element of care, the hairdresser comes into close contact with her clients, but her touch can't be compared to that of a doctor because people seeing a doctor are often scared or anxious. The hairdresser will place her hands on the shoulders of an old client and make eye contact with her in the mirror: There, don't you look nice now. If the hairdresser asks Mum about her family in a sensitive way, Mum will say that she has a daughter who has four children. Ruth's four children are grown up and have interesting jobs and relationships Mum can talk about. No one would suspect that anyone has been left out, it has become a habit. Mum no longer feels a pang in her heart as she did in the first few years when her older daughter couldn't be mentioned.

Perhaps Mum has started talking about her mother, who died young, whom I never met, whom she never talked about, she was probably a *remarkable* woman.

But what if I happened to book an appointment at Mum's salon, it's theoretically possible. Then I would sit, as I sat the other day, with my eyes trained on the newspaper while what I was really doing was listening to what Mum told her hairdresser about her grandchildren, whose names I don't know. And what if she were to start talking about having no contact with her older daughter, because a salon might just be conducive to such confessions? Mum can't talk to Ruth about me. It has been years since Ruth got fed up with hearing about me, since Mum stopped mentioning me to Ruth who probably said: *Thinking about her does you no good.* Nor does Mum talk to her older brother about me, according to 1881, he is still alive and lives with his wife in Tranbygd, because if Mum had told him that I had called and that she hadn't answered the phone, he might hint that she ought to have done. But her hairdresser won't because the hairdresser's job is to be polite and sympathetic no matter what the client says, perhaps the salon is the only place where Mum feels safe to talk about me. What does Mum say about me to her hairdresser? Should I find out where she goes and make an appointment there?

In the house where I grew up and the house we moved to when I was in my early teens, there were several photographs of Ruth and me on the large antique bureau in the living room. A black-and-white photo of each daughter on her third birthday, taken by a professional photographer. We had bows in our hair to keep our fringes out of the way. Confirmation pictures and then wedding photographs followed, first Thorleif and me in front of the old stone church, then Ruth and Reidar in front of the same church, the summer before I left.

Did Mum and Dad take down the pictures of me at that point? I'm thinking no. It would look strange to those who were regular visitors to the house, drastic and melodramatic, besides everyone thought I would be back soon. I was in crisis and had lost my way, but I would come to my senses eventually and find my way home, I assume that was what they were hoping, all except Ruth possibly. And if I didn't come to my senses, then the no-good Mark would invariably leave me and I would turn up with my tail between my legs on the doorstep of my childhood home. No, the pictures of me probably stayed where they were for a while, but when Dad died fourteen years ago and Mum moved to a new flat, the pictures of me did not come with her.

I was sitting at Borg station after a meeting with the curator when an old woman came up the stairs. She took one heavy step at a time and clung to the handrail in order not to fall and break her hip. Safe on the platform, she began rummaging in her handbag and a handkerchief fell out, she bent down with an effort to retrieve it, carried on searching, found what she was looking for, a piece of paper, peered at it, resumed going through her bag, found her glasses, took them out of their case and put them on, dropped the case, stared at the piece of paper and shook her head. She looked about her, I was the only other person on the platform, she came towards me on unsteady legs, held up the note and asked which train she needed to catch. I had to find my own glasses in my own handbag in order to read it, it was the name of a doctor's surgery. I asked if she had been there before, she shook her head, pointed to her ear, I might need a hearing aid, she said in a voice so loud that I concluded she certainly did. Didn't she have anyone to take her? It's in Broholmen, she said, then you're on the right platform, I said, you need to travel that way, I said, the opposite direction from me, fortunately, there was her train. Your train, I said, I picked up the glasses case and gave it to her, the train stopped and she boarded it, two stops, I said, she nodded vigorously and repeated: Two stops! She either had no children or she had fallen out with them.

Ruth takes Mum to the doctor's. Or her adult children do, they probably love their grandmother. That night I dreamt about the woman at the station, I dreamt that I put her on the wrong train and she travelled on it to its final destination as quiet as a mouse, with thinning hair and sunken cheeks and she sat so slumped that no one noticed her and the train driver got off and disappeared into the night and she was left all alone and defenceless: Mum!

Do I imagine Mum confused and helpless at a railway station to beat myself up? Does it make me feel good or do I torment myself imagining Mum confused on a platform? Mum has Ruth and Ruth's big family. Ruth probably still works, but she is not as ambitious as she used to be and she has time to help Mum. Here I go again, telling myself Ruth was never ambitious, why do I do that? I don't know her, she was in her early twenties when I left, but I reckon I would have heard if she had achieved something noteworthy in her field, I can't find anything on the Internet. I tell myself it's because she never stood up to Mum and Dad, never said out loud that she disagreed with their views, regardless of what they were, it looked as if she liked or she pretended to like their rules and wanted to live the way they lived. But is agreeing with your parents' rules incompatible with having a career? On the contrary, many successful people follow the rules of their family and society in everything and that's why they succeed. I imagine Ruth lacking ambition because I want her to have time to care for Mum, so I don't feel guilty for having gone away and left my parents to her, so she couldn't contemplate travelling or breaking away because someone had to take Mum to the doctor's and more and more often now because Mum is ageing. And Ruth is ageing as I am, as is everyone on this earth with each year.

I can paint the ageing daughter taking her old mother to the doctor's, *Child and Mother 3*. I go to the studio and stretch out a canvas, I look at it, a canvas ready to prime, then I leave. It's Sunday, I call John.

I don't know what Ruth does for a living, I googled her, but I didn't find anything. She was at Oslo Business School when I left, many companies and organisations need people with financial skills. I tell myself she lives a conventional life, that she doesn't travel much for work because she has four children and Mum. I bumped into a childhood friend of hers at Heathrow airport some years ago, I was having a cup of coffee when a woman stopped and asked if I was Johanna, Ruth's sister, I went red. When she said her name, Regina Madsen, I could make out a childhood face behind the now mature one, she had lived right across the street from us, and she, too, had been scared of Mrs Benzen. I couldn't get away, which was what I instinctively wanted to do; I was face to face with someone who had the answers to many of my questions about my family, but I couldn't ask them. Showing an interest now would have seemed indecent when for all those years I hadn't appeared to care. She seemed to realise that I didn't know anything about Ruth's life, and that it would be awkward for me to have to ask. Unprompted she then told me that Ruth and Reidar and their children were all well, and all four of the kids had left home. As it happened, she had just spoken to Ruth because Ruth's daughter, Randi, now lived in London and Regina Madsen had had lunch with her that very day! She told me things like that, but nothing more, weighing her words carefully, saying too much

54

would be a betrayal of Ruth. She asked me a few questions in the same reserved manner, how old was my son, she knew I had a son. When I said he was a viola player, she was surprised and said something about the apple and the tree and then she fell silent, but I sensed she wanted to probe further, that had it been up to her, she would have asked many more questions, but to show curiosity would be an admission on Ruth's behalf, as if Ruth cared.

I was six years old when my sister was born. I barely remember her as a baby and toddler. She was there, of course, but in the background somehow, in Mum's or Dad's arms. We never went to the same school, I struggle to recall images of us together, not even from the long summers we spent in the cabin in Rondane. When I think back on them, I remember the sheep and the foxes better than I do her; she exists in a blurred periphery. I hope that's not unusual when the age gap is so big. Did I play with the twins from the cabin across the lake, while she was on her own with Mum and Dad? I don't remember. Did Regina Madsen ever tell Ruth that she had met me at Heathrow, I'm guessing she did. And that John was a viola player, Ruth was probably surprised at that, but she still didn't get the answer to what she most wanted to know, which Regina couldn't tell her anything about, which was how was I with the *situation*?

Ruth's number is unlisted. So that I can't call. She is angry with me because once I'd gone, she couldn't take a job which involved leaving Oslo or do much travelling. Perhaps she was offered an exciting job in London, but turned it down because of Mum and Dad. Ruth's life had been constrained through and by my actions, and once Dad died, Mum became dependent on her. Mum didn't drive a car back when I knew her, she was always a very impractical person, needing help with most things, and she wasn't the type to refrain from asking, on the contrary, she regarded it as her right, given what she had done for Ruth as a child and paid for everything, what kind of leisure activities did Ruth do, I don't remember. But might Mum's older brother, Tor, who according to 1881 is alive and lives with someone called Toril Gran, be able to help? No, they live in Tranbygd two hundred kilometres away and keep themselves to themselves. Mum is reluctant to ask Tor, they were never close, she displays her boundless neediness mostly to her children, that is to say Ruth. But Mum talks to Tor on the phone and he is useful in that way, old people spend a lot of time talking on the phone to the still living. Or perhaps they have fallen out, siblings do. And the cousin from Hamar with whom she grew up, Grethe, who was widowed so long ago that Mum didn't find it difficult to call me to let me know, she probably sees her. I was sitting on a bench by the river, my phone rang, I saw it was a Norwegian number, I recognised it and my pulse quickened, I answered it thinking Mum was ringing clandestinely without Dad or Ruth knowing. She adopted a mournful tone of voice and said that Halvor had died. I didn't remember who Halvor was, my cousin Grethe's husband, she said, and I remembered him and I asked how, a sudden heart attack. There was silence, then she told me Ruth was pregnant. How nice, I said. Ruth was seven months pregnant with a boy who would be named Rolf after Dad, the names of all their children would start with R. Ruth and Reidar had bought a house not far from Mum and Dad, they saw them several times a week. It all felt very far away and remote. She didn't ask about John.

I could go to Arne Bruns gate 22 and bump into her there, but it would be unpleasant for Mum when she isn't prepared, as it would also be for me.

According to 1881, Mum's cousin Grethe now lives within walking distance of Mum. They probably see each other often. They take the Metro to Vassbuseter and go for walks in the forests I don't visit for fear of bumping into them. Instead I have a forest of my own, I have rented a log cabin in Bumarken where I won't bump into anyone. It's a twenty-minute walk from the car park and so far the only creature I've met is an elk. I work well there, I draw trees. Mum and Grethe walk from Vassbuseter to Groleitet to drink hot chocolate, they aren't watching their weight anymore. Or perhaps they have fallen out, cousins do even when they are old. Mum and Grethe walk from Vassbuseter to Groleitet, if they haven't fallen out that is, and if they don't need a Zimmer frame. The Zimmer frame happens to us all sooner or later, we age towards the Zimmer frame. Mina's mum used a Zimmer frame in the final year of her life, but she was fat. I hope Mum isn't fat. Mina's mum would walk at a snail's pace, her hands gripping the handles of the Zimmer frame, her knuckles white, she moved like an injured insect, the death of a moth, the death of a fly, equally prosaic. In the basket at the front of the frame was a crossword puzzle, a packet of paper tissues, a roll of biscuits and her medication, the grey hair on the back of her head was matted. Old people forget to brush the back of their head, the backs of old people's heads make me think of their beds, why is that a sad image? A few times when I was a child I brushed Mum's long, copper-red hair, it was an honour, but too intimate. Does Ruth brush Mum's hair, are they that intimate? Does Ruth know Mum's smell, and does she like it?

I've inherited Mum's colouring. Red hair and freckles, a carrot top.

Do Ruth's children know about me? She can't have omitted to tell them that she has a sister. They know she has one, but they don't ask about her, they sense it's a sore point. Am I a sore point? No, who cares about an old aunt. If Ruth or Mum *has* to talk about me because Grethe inadvertently mentions my name at Mum's eighty-fifth birthday, which is happening one of these days, and Ruth's children ask who is that – what do they say? I'm guessing the story goes like this: Johanna was a promising law student, married to a solid and dependable lawyer, Thorleif Rød, but in the spring of 1990, she joined a watercolour evening class, fell head over heels in love with her American tutor Mark something or other, and ran off with him. When Grandad fell ill, she didn't come home, nor did she come to his funeral. Shame on her. And that's the end of that. Or like this: Johanna was mentally unstable and capricious ever since she was little, she gave in to every whim and urge she ever had without thinking of the consequences for others or for herself. She didn't turn up for Grandad's funeral. Shame on her. That's all there is to it. Nothing about my art, which they probably don't regard as art, but as a vendetta. That's why they don't take an interest in art, it's not art just because no one understands it, ha-ha. So if Ruth's children don't know my new surname, and why would someone have told them, they won't be able to look up my work and activities on the Internet, but why should they.

Doesn't something about these stories grate? Would a child who loved her parents behave like this? Yes, a few would irrespective of anything their parents had done, young women especially can become so infatuated with a man that they cut all previous ties in order to be with him. It's probably M who won't let Johanna have any contact with her family, they don't know that he is dead. Mum has said this so many times to other people that she must believe it herself, but if that's the case then she would have picked up the phone when I finally called! And she didn't. So it *is* about my work, which shames them the way they see it, the triptych *Child and Mother 1* where the mother stands in a corner wrapped up in herself with dark, introverted eyes and the child is curled up in the other corner, and those who want to can see that the shadow falling over both of them looks like a man in a lawyer's gown. I could only have painted it in Utah, eight thousand kilometres away, that's why I moved to Utah eight thousand kilometres away. Initially when the invitation to exhibit in the city of my childhood arrived, I didn't want to do it, but Mark persuaded me. My paintings had been successful in Germany, Canada and Japan, and nobody who had written about them had suggested that the mother must be based on the artist's own mother, it was the generic mother who was the subject, and that explained why so many people could relate to it, because when you create something based on your own experiences, it will often resonate with many others, Mark said, he didn't know Mum and Dad. For them the risk that their neighbours and acquaintances *might* view the pictures as a message from the daughter across the sea was in itself a betrayal. That I had painted the pictures without wondering: What will Mum and Dad think? The question every child ought to ask itself before it acts. Like Dad would invariably consult his own mother's powerful voice inside him before he made a decision. Dad chose the burden of following the fourth commandment, while I chose freedom and had the nerve not to obey Mum's and Dad's voices in me. They never acknowledged that I had painted the pictures to ensure my own survival.

But worst of all, Dad died, and I didn't go to his funeral.

I defend myself as though I were under attack. Is it because I don't take Mum's reaction, Mum's suffering seriously, but only my own? We are closest to our own suffering. But I suspect that mine is deeply linked to hers, which was so secret, I've always had a strong sense of it.

I call Mum, she doesn't pick up. I email Ruth. Are you telling Mum not to talk to me? Ruth doesn't reply.

I write: If Mum says she doesn't want to talk to me, I'll accept it, but if you're behind this, you must realise that it's a huge responsibility to take on. I reveal to Ruth my belief that Mum would pick up the phone if she could choose freely. I want to hear it from Mum herself. Ruth doesn't reply, there is silence. What had I expected and how would I react if Mum had texted me: I don't want to talk to you ever again.

I tell myself that if she were to put it as brutally as that then I would accept it and find peace.

I find peace in my log cabin, I spend more and more time there.

September 20, I sit on the doorstep. For three days in a row the elk has appeared and ambled with calm dignity across the mound as if I weren't there, but yesterday it stopped at the crooked birch, turned its head in my direction and looked straight at me. I didn't move a muscle. If it started charging at me, I had time to run inside and close the door, but why would it do that? For more than a minute it stood still, gazing at me with black, reflective eyes before it resumed its lumbering walk and disappeared in between the trees. In the evening I walked along the road before it grew dark, in the grass by the barrier I found small chanterelles, I let them be, the peace of the forest.

I think about the elk's black eyes and draw its heavy, earth-bound gait with artist's charcoal, I can submit charcoal drawings to the retrospective. I go outside and lie down on the ground, I close my eyes and start to feel an intense, physical contact with the knobbly moss underneath me, the damp from the ground seeps slowly into my anorak and trousers and I get wet, I sink into myself as I feel the heavy wetness of the earth draw me near, and I realise it's not the sky we should be facing, but the earth.

When I sat in front of the fire, I called Mum, it was easier now, as if a barrier had been broken, my anxiety lessened, my call was rejected, yet again I emailed Ruth: Have you deleted my number on Mum's phone? I showed Ruth that I believed Mum would have picked up the phone if she had been *allowed* to, that Mum really wants to talk to me, that it's a huge temptation. That Mum has a hope pinned on me which must be balanced against her fear of Ruth. She can't have succeeded in killing me off to the extent that she no longer wonders how I am. But I already know she won't pick up, I've tried that before and yet I ring.

If Mum had asked me to come back when Dad was ill, if Mum had called and asked me in her own voice to come home for Dad's funeral, would I have gone? I tell myself I would. But Ruth communicated with me on Mum's behalf, and Ruth didn't ask me to come. Perhaps Mum asked Ruth to ask me to come, but Ruth didn't pass on the message because she didn't want me there.

I blame Ruth so that Mum can go free, it's simpler that way.

Ruth doesn't reply, Ruth is silent and I'm unable to work. I text Ruth that there is something I *have* to say to Mum. I don't know what it is, but Ruth can't know what it is either. It might have to do with John, but why would they care about someone they have never met? Ruth doesn't reply. She thinks that if I *need* to speak to Mum, then I can write Mum a letter and post it. However, in order to spare Mum, Ruth will want to know the contents of such a letter before she lets Mum read it. And so Ruth regularly checks Mum's post. Ruth has keys for Mum's flat and Mum's post box, but Ruth has to go to work and when will the postman call and when will Mum pick up her post, logistically it's a tricky challenge she has set herself. I imagine that she leaves work in her lunch break, lets herself into Arne Bruns gate 22 and checks Mum's post box in the hope of finding a letter from me containing what?

I'm no minor character. They would both tear open a letter from me with trembling hands. Because I'm the daughter, the sister, because we are mythological beings to one another, and because we are enemies, who isn't curious about their enemy? But they don't respond to my approaches, their resentment outweighs their curiosity. And who do I think I am. I shit on my own doorstep, then I call as if nothing has happened. Do I think Mum has no pride? I must factor in pride.

I sit in the log cabin and I can sense that the elk wants something from me. It turns up every day around two o'clock, it wanders the same route across the mound, creating a path past the dead pine tree, but it always stops in the same spot by my friend the stone and looks at me. It rained earlier today and I thought it wouldn't come, then the rain stopped, a blackbird sang, a double rainbow arched over the vast sky, and the elk came.

Ruth didn't take me seriously when I wrote I had important information for Mum, and she was right, but on an existential level I'm right because I do have something important to tell her although I can't find the words and don't know what it is yet. It doesn't belong in the rational sphere.

I sit on the balcony and look down at the big maples below, a few crumpled leaves are still attached to the delicate but tough branches, they look like Chinese lanterns without candles.

Mum gets up and turns on her coffee machine. While she waits for the coffee to percolate, she goes to the hallway, opens the door and picks up the newspaper from the doormat, she still subscribes to a print newspaper. She brings it into the kitchen and finds the obituary page, Mum's gateway to the *Aftenposten*. I hope she doesn't turn on the TV. Ruth has made sure she has every channel, perhaps Mum has the television on from morning till night, I hope not. I have Mum turn on the radio while she waits for her coffee to brew. I turn on the radio, I wait for my coffee to brew.

From her kitchen table Mum can see trees, but not the ones I can see from the cabin, pines, spruces and some crooked birches. The trees on the picture on 1881 look like the ones I can see when I stand on the balcony outside the studio and look down, maples someone has planted, I decide that Mum can see trees from her kitchen table where she is now sitting. I decide that she eats crispbread with butter and goat's cheese with her coffee, the leaves she looks at have only just started to turn yellow, and the sun shines on them and on her as it shines on me. In between the foliage, the sky is as blue to her as it is to me and it's mindboggling that we are both looking at it. Mum drinks her hot coffee in small sips, but doesn't read the rest of her newspaper, it doesn't interest her as it did in the old days, in fact it never has, but the TV listings are at the back. Then her phone, which lies near her on the table, rings, it's Ruth, she usually calls at this time of the morning. She asks if Mum has slept well and Mum tells her about her night and what her plans are for today, and they both feel better when the conversation is over. It's good to talk to someone you care about. The day can begin. Mum is meeting Rigmor, who is also widowed, they meet regularly at the patisserie in Sous Plass. Mum looks forward to chatting with Rigmor, both have recently had a doctor's appointment. I imagine that they have come to terms with their ageing bodies, that they laugh at themselves when they happen to leave their spectacles in the fridge, but also that it scares them. They don't talk about their fear, I think. They talk about their children and grandchildren and show one another pictures on their mobile phones. Ruth's children are not yet old enough for Mum to have great-grandchildren, I think, she has just the one, John's Erik, but she doesn't know about him. They talk about the old days, they remember the dead, more have died since they last met. They joke that soon it will be their turn. But deep down they are terrified. They don't talk about their terror either, nor do they talk about me. They spend a long time at the patisserie eating cake. Or they don't eat cake because it's bad for their cholesterol and they want to live long in the land. Afterwards they go shopping, it is always someone's birthday and it's a joy to treat the grandchildren. Before they go their separate ways, they hug one another, then Mum walks home in high spirits and tired in a good way, and unpacks her bits and pieces.

The sky is high, the nights are cool, the air smells of roots and leaves, a grouse chirps, a glossy cobweb shimmers in the sunshine, the world rests, it feels like I am of the earth and not of Mum.

Mum has enjoyed her retail therapy with Rigmor. Mum has no financial problems, Mum doesn't worry about money or the environment. I don't think she checks where an item was produced or what it is made of in order to determine its environmental footprint before she buys it. That's just my assumption. Mum never took an interest in politics or social issues as far as I can recall and that's why I keep telling myself that our *situation* must trouble her because it belongs in the domestic sphere. But Mum doesn't want to discuss it, not even with Rigmor, because an estrangement between a mother and a daughter can't ever be the fault of just one party, can it? Questions about the cause could also prove awkward even if Mum tries to blame our estrangement on the power M has over me, she doesn't know that he is dead. But I'm guessing Rigmor shares Mum's view of my paintings as disgraceful. Rigmor thanks God that she doesn't have a daughter who is an artist. And besides, I failed to turn up for Dad's funeral.

But how did I become so inconsiderate, so heartless? No one asks so as not to ruin the mood. Deep insight isn't Mum and her friends' strong point. They know that she no longer sends birthday cards to her grandson, my son, but that's my fault.

Mum, I use words to create my image of you.

Violets and wild pansies still grow along the lanes, above me the sky is pale blue though the ridges on the horizon are black and sharply outlined against the low red clouds in the west, rosebay willow herb grows among the scree where vipers warm themselves in the evening sun and behind it raspberry canes mingle with lush ferns and further up the valley puddles glitter on the moors and golden rays of sunshine fall on the moss where I sit, lingonberries grow on old tree stumps, and blueberry slopes and patches of funnel chanterelles nestle in the shadow of the spruces behind me and the sound of sheep bells is coming closer, it's nice, but it's not the elk. What kind of landscape am I venturing into, perhaps it's not healthy? A birthday card? Do I project my issues onto my *son*, with all the associations of someone vulnerable and defenceless that word implies, in order to make Mum appear heartless? Has my *son* ever indicated that he minded not getting a birthday card from his Norwegian grandmother, no. But even if he minded, would he have told me? Has John never shown any interest in his Norwegian family because he picked up on my reticence, just as Rigmor doesn't ask Mum about me because she senses her reluctance? But I have told John about what I call the conflict or the estrangement. That Mum and Dad disagreed with my choice of profession and spouse, had taken it badly that I left suddenly and that I later exhibited paintings they didn't like, but I have never shown him the paintings, in order not to burden him with my problems. Or is that to make my life easy? What if I haven't shown them to him because I fear that he might recognise me as the mother turning away, completely wrapped up in herself? But I was never anything like Mum! I didn't interfere and I didn't wish for anything on John's behalf, I never had any expectations, probably because of what I myself had gone through, but maybe John missed more involvement, greater participation from me, so was I ultimately as useless a mum as my mum – except mine was a sin of omission – because it would be naive to think that Mum's pain had turned into my anxiety without my pain turning into John's burden. But if he ever wants to talk to me or pour out his heart in a letter as I did to Mum and Dad, I would be open and prostrate! But I don't want Mum to prostrate herself, I just want us to have an honest conversation, and anyway the relationship between mother and son and mother and daughter is different, because the mother is a mirror in which the daughter sees her future self and the daughter is a mirror in which the mother sees her lost self, and so maybe Mum doesn't want to see me so she won't know what she has lost? A child may have to rebel against its parents in order to discover its own will and find its own path, and if the parents can accept that, the family members can ultimately establish a more equal relationship because everyone proved naked and vulnerable in the heat of battle, and because they tried to articulate complicated and ambivalent feelings, something which Mum and I never did. And that has to happen in order to break the vicious cycle of pain, is that what I'm trying to do?

Surely parents have the lifelong obligation, unlike the child? According to the Bible, it's the other way round, the child must honour its mother and father in order to live long in the land, but then again the Bible was written by parents to keep the offspring in their place.

I call John. He doesn't pick up. Later he texts me to say he was on a plane to Vienna where he will be playing in the Gesellschaft der Musikfreunde. I'm proud of him, I text him. I text that he must never be scared of addressing difficult issues. He replies with an emoji with a crooked smile.

Mum lets herself into her flat, she sets down her shopping bags, sits down on a chair and kicks off her shoes. She is tired now, happy but tired. What time is it? Maybe six o'clock in late September, the birds have begun to settle in the trees, it's starting to grow dark earlier, a kind of shadow is already approaching the balcony where she goes out because she wants to watch the birds, the migrating ones and the loyal grey ones that stay. I haven't seen a single human being for the four days I've been here, just birds, sheep and the elk. Perhaps she has a glass of wine on her balcony, she no longer has any fear of dependency. Even the doctors say she should have a glass or two whenever she wants to. I go in, open a bottle, pour myself a glass and return to the doorstep, I can smell the tar in the sun-warmed timber, I lean against it, the sheep bells approach slowly, it's nice when they pass by, but it's not the same as the elk.

Fifty-three kilometres from where I'm sitting.

Mum snoozes on her balcony. She enjoys sitting there in the late afternoon sunshine, she can see the sun's red ball between the tall, still leafy trees. But then she checks her watch, gets up and goes to her bedroom where there is a single bed? Ruth has helped Mum buy furniture, perhaps they chose a double bed because Mum has slept in one her entire adult life and just in case she got herself a new boyfriend, Pax's aunt met a new man when she was eighty-one and I believe she is happy. Mum and Ruth probably bought a single bed, 1.2 metres wide, and some new bed linens. Buying new bed linens is a symbolic act. They must have thrown many things away when they cleared out the big house, cleared out Dad and what remained of me, how therapeutic it must have been. They cleared out Dad's things with loving hands, caressing suits and ties and sniffing old jumpers, caps, scarves, smoothing and folding them with reverence and placing them in boxes they then took to the Salvation Army, shoes, socks, underwear, a human being leaves behind so much. The Salvation Army is a good thing, others now walk around in Dad's suits and shoes, I wonder if I've passed one of Dad's suits in the street. Mum might have kept a few mementos, his wedding ring and his watch, in her bedside drawer, does she open it at night, look at them and think of Dad? I don't think so. How strange it must be to have lived for so long with another human being, so close to them, day after day, night after night, year after year, then one of you dies and turns to dust. I've heard that animals that live in close proximity invariably grow fond of each other and that people who do the same might equally well end up hating one another. Did Mum ever have anything resembling a deep conversation with Dad? No, that would have been too risky. They stuck to safe subjects, Ruth's children, Dad's job, the varieties of roses in the garden, there was a certain distance even back when I knew them, then Dad died and Mum misses someone with whom she can talk about flowers. Mum threw away the old bed linens and the old towels and bought new ones, her new life in her new flat was about to begin. I still have a set of bed linens from my childhood home. I ended up with it by chance when I first left home and since then it has travelled everywhere with me. A few more items from my childhood have followed me for inexplicable reasons and I still have them, have they become too symbolic to throw away? An ornate brass ashtray from Dad's time in the Netherlands, some little teak plates he made in woodwork as a child along with a clothes hanger with his name burned into it. They can't write me out of the story, I have proof. These objects can only be in my possession because I grew up in his house. They are worthless, dead items, why don't I just throw them out, I never use the bed linens from my childhood home when I make up a bed. But neither did I throw them away when I moved here, I'll do so when I return from the forest, I stay in the cabin the whole weekend.

Mum undresses. She places her clothes on a chair, is it at this moment she feels most alone? She is pale, she has yet to go abroad for some winter sun, I remember Mum's white skin, the freckles on her chest, her tanned cheeks all those summers in the mountains, she changes into her pyjamas and then a cash-mere cardigan which isn't folded, but hangs on a hanger. Mum puts on her slippers and goes to the living room, sits down in her favourite armchair and turns on the television, she watches a documentary about African wildlife. It's reassuring, that's why I have her watch it. Elegant antelopes with white bellies grazing under a vast, pale blue Kenyan sky, the sun shines on the plains, which are the same colour as the animals. It's warm there while it grows colder here, autumn is coming, anyone who has lived through many autumns will recognise it. Mum longs for warm weather, but doesn't want to go to Africa, Africa is best on the telly, but I can't know that for sure, perhaps Ruth took Mum and all of her big family on a safari in Africa when Mum turned eighty, and so the documentary makes Mum remember the time they shared a tent in the Serengeti. The antelopes graze calmly on the savannah; the camera zooms in on a pride of lions in the shade of an acacia tree. Two females lazing on their sides, their fur the colour of the dry grass, four cubs playing, the male nearby, his head held high. Then back to the grazing antelopes, the sound track plays Sunday morning mood music, but we are not fooled because the lionesses have got up and are creeping through the grass, the music changes to sinister night, one lioness approaches the herd, the other sneaks around it in a semicircle, she runs like a shadow through the tall grass, the herd senses her and starts moving, a grey cloud on the savannah sky, pity the slowest antelope that makes up the tail end of this cloud. Don't lead, said the mother to her son who was going off to war, and don't linger at the back, walk in the middle, those who walk in the middle come back, but how can the calf, on which the camera is now zooming in, get to the middle when the others run faster and don't come to her rescue, I think it's a female. The other lioness makes a beeline for the calf, hunting as they do in pairs, jumps onto its back and bites down, the antelope continues to run, the other lioness arrives and sinks her teeth into the throat of the antelope, two lionesses on its body, the antelope's legs run more slowly until they collapse, the blood is pouring from its wounds, especially the one to the throat, this is for the benefit of the lion cubs. Its white belly slams onto the ground, the lioness that rode it jumps off and both of them bite its throat, the antelope's eyes bulge, black and terrified, its body trembles, it's not dead yet, the lion cubs come bouncing along happily, Dad eats first, Mum turns off the TV.

She gets up, perhaps with effort, perhaps with ease, goes to the bathroom and watches her face in the mirror as she brushes her teeth. She loosens her hair and it falls over her shoulders, I don't think she has had it cut short, it may have gone grey, but then she dyes it because so much of her identity is tied up in her red hair, the flame from Hamar. Mum goes to the kitchen, pours herself a glass of water and shuffles barefoot to the bedroom, she sits down on the side of the bed, pops a sleeping pill into her mouth, drinks some water, swallows it, lies down and packs the duvet around herself as she has done every single night since Dad died. I'm interested in this moment. The half hour before the pill kicks in. Mum in bed. Waiting, thinking. About what? The day that has just ended. The day tomorrow, her hairdresser's appointment. And after that then what?

Ruth helped Mum decide what would come with her to the new flat and what to throw away. I'm guessing they threw away anything that might remind them of me, they wouldn't want to display like a wound my confirmation and wedding photographs and the picture of my new-born son. I imagine Ruth chucking them out and the glass smashing as it hits the bottom of the skip. No, I'm not worth that much emotion. She just drops them indifferently into a bin bag and takes it to a dump.

When Ruth realised that I had come home, she told Mum so Mum would be prepared if I were to contact her or if she happened to bump into me. But once she had done that, then what? Stay silent as they have been silent about me all these years, or relive what they regard as my betrayal and feel resentful together, I'm guessing I was constantly present as a source of outrage during my absence. How would they suppress the alarm which the news of my return has probably induced?

It's night-time now. Mum sleeps fitfully.

I explore areas of the city where I expect they don't go. The city has grown, my chances of bumping into Ruth or Mum are small. Except possibly at Oslo Central Station. Mum never liked public transport, but she has to use it now when Ruth can't drive her. When I visit museums in the morning, I'm mindful that they are popular with old people, but Mum avoids art galleries because of me. Just to be on the safe side I make sure I sit in cafés so that I can see who comes and goes, and I always have an escape plan. When I was at the counter at the Arts and Crafts Museum café the other day, a woman tapped me on my shoulder and asked if I was me, I couldn't deny it. She knew Mum's brother, Tor, she said, they had worked together for the Red Cross and he had told her that I, the artist, was his niece. She said it as if it wasn't something Tor was ashamed of. She asked if I had moved back to Norway, I hesitated. Tor had broken his wrist, she said, but perhaps I already knew? And I felt embarrassed, and she looked at me quizzically, but he was OK now, she said. The barista asked if I would be drinking my coffee here or if I wanted it to go, I took it with me and left.

So Mum's brother Tor talks about me. Also to Mum? Does Tor visit Mum and comment on the photographs of me no longer being on display? Or does he know it will make her uncomfortable and so refrains? But he *notices*. Perhaps Mum gets upset merely on hearing my name and so everyone around her avoids saying it. Perhaps Mum feels uneasy every time she hears the name even if it's just some random Johanna, a skier or a newsreader, the name is mentioned and Mum shudders, Mum is lucky that not many people are called Johanna. Perhaps Mum has succeeded in suppressing unpleasant thoughts about me in her everyday life – she has years of practice – but then it pops up in a random interviewee on the television whose name is Johanna, and Mum feels nauseous, turns off the television with a pounding heart, and calls my sister to ease her mind.

They can't cross me off the family tree.

Mum lives in Arne Bruns gate 22. I found a picture of her apartment block on 1881. I know this part of town, but not well, I might have passed through it on a bus, I've never been to Arne Bruns gate itself, as far as I know. It's a red brick building. Now I can picture it in my mind, that's all I need. I go to the log cabin in the forest to increase the distance. The leaves have turned brick red, but summer still lives in the timber, summer lingers in the timber until late October, the sun penetrates the tarred logs, which on the inside are the colour of freshly-baked bread and human skin, the sun lives in the wood for as long as it can, the logs soak up the rays and the warmth, the cabin is warm as I let myself in. Driving there from the cabin will take me on another route. An expedition with a different starting point, almost as if someone else were doing it. I don't know what Mum's week looks like, but I'm guessing that her diary isn't full, I'm guessing that Ruth's week looks like that of most employees, I'm guessing that Mum goes out alone if she goes out on a Tuesday morning. The weather is nice, that's a reason to go outside. Autumn is the best time of year, the light is clear, the air sharp against your face, even when the sun warms it. If a cloud covers the sun, it gets cold immediately, but when the cloud has passed and the sun reappears, it warms the mind and the heart. Mum doesn't know what kind of car I drive, Mum isn't interested in cars, I think, I constantly have to add an 'I think'. Yet I don't want to park too close, I want to park so that I can see who comes out of her building, but not so close that they will notice me. People tend not to sit in parked cars. You will only wait in your car if you are picking someone up and you get there too early, but then you don't turn off the ignition, you don't parallel park, you signal and pull over. Someone sitting in a parked car for a long time is an unusual sight, but it's also so unusual that no one would be looking for anyone doing that. It belongs in the realm of spy movies. When I'm out walking, I never check to see if people are sitting in the cars I pass, my gaze is trained straight ahead. And if I were to see someone in a parked car, I would expect the car to pull out soon or the person to get out and leave. But if I saw someone sitting in a parked car for a long time as if it was somewhere to stay, would I find it strange or sinister? Not if that person was studying a map. And so I pack a map, I plan this as though it were a crime. If I can't find somewhere to park, I'll just drive round the block and try again. Perhaps I'll have to drive round many times, that wouldn't be unusual in a street so relatively close to the city centre. If I still can't find a space, I'll turn back, there's no shame in turning back. I don't smile, my hand is trembling in September. Once the sun goes down behind the spruce trees, it soon grows cold, I light a fire in the wood burner in the kitchen and in the sturdy brick fireplace in the small living room and walk down to the unlit main road to calm my mind, I follow it for one kilometre, it's not so dark that I can't see where I'm going, I can hear sheep bells. I detect no light coming from any of the other cabins on the hillside, but on my way back I see the light from my own and welcoming smoke rising from the chimney, it calms me down, my heart and my brain are restless, it's warm as I enter.

~

It's a forty-minute drive from here. Had I left straight from the flat, it would have taken me half the time, but it would have been a different experience. From here it's an expedition, a route I've never driven before. First the deserted roads, then the traffic slowly starts to build up as I approach the city and arrive at the motorway from an unaccustomed direction, then I turn off. I drive with my heart in my throat, my pulse throbbing as I approach, I don't know what I'm doing, that's the whole point, to find out. I was more mindful when I got into the car, whatever happens I'll learn something about myself, I'm excited to find out what it might be. I drive slowly, I irritate those behind me, I prolong it, then suddenly and surprisingly I'm there as if – because driving there has been mentally exhausting – I had expected it to be hard to find, but it isn't, I've already gone past it, an undramatic location with many places to park, but I don't reverse, I drive round the block and re-enter the street more slowly and pass number 22, a red brick building with an ordinary entrance, I drive around the block again and enter Arne Bruns gate for the third time, past the red brick apartment block I notice a vacant spot outside a similar building farther down, I drive past it, I turn around at the junction, drive back and park so I can see Mum's building in front of me to the right, approximately twenty metres farther ahead. My legs are trembling, what am I doing here, I don't know, I'm waiting for Mum. She is alive and breathing less than a hundred metres away from me, if she is at home, if she is alive; if she were dead, I would have been told. The building is asleep. There are square wooden flower boxes painted blue on either side of the entrance, they signal something formal, but there is nothing to suggest that it is anything other than private apartments spread over five floors, I don't know which one Mum lives in. If there is a lift, it could be any of them, there probably is a lift, the building looks newly renovated. Ten large balconies face the street, all filled with flowers. But there are balconies at the ends as well and, I'm guessing, also at the back, Mum's balcony could face the street where I'm sitting, but also a neighbouring block, they all look as if they were built around the same time, early twentieth century, renovated many times since, it is a nice area. I can see no sign of life in the windows facing me, but then who looks out of their window and down at the sleepy street at this time of day, it's five minutes past ten in the morning. No people, no moving cars. I slide as far down the seat as I can, but it soon becomes uncomfortable, I straighten up as much as I dare, I don't turn on the radio although I tell myself it's not dangerous, it still feels dangerous. I don't unfold the map lying next to me as there is no one to do it for. I sit tense, sensing my own breathing for an hour, I'm thinking I should be going when a woman comes towards me. It's not Mum, it's not a woman over eighty, I can see that immediately, one single look and I know that it's not a woman over eighty, that it's not Mum, that it's a woman my age, Ruth? It can't be, she doesn't look like my sister, and besides she walks straight past Arne Bruns gate 22 as if she doesn't know that she is walking down Mum's street. My sister knows this street, my sister lives seventeen minutes away on foot, I've checked on 1881, but she probably drives there in her car as I do, she is at work now. But if contrary to expectation she were to drive here to visit Mum on a Tuesday morning for some reason, she wouldn't focus on the cars already parked, but on any vacant spaces, like the one in front of me, but my sister doesn't come. A dog appears, apparently ownerless, it sniffs the lamp post in front of me, then relieves itself before it disappears. I sit there for two and a half hours, then I drive back to the forest, my body feels lethargic. I stop at the flat ground near the dense spruce forest and walk until darkness falls, I roam around and I find sweet tooth mushrooms that glow creamy yellow against the dark ground, and I return to the car with a bag full. When I park in my usual space, it is so dark that I can't see the path between the trees, I have forgotten to switch on the cabin's external lights. It is pitch black, the air is acidic and the heather autumn-crisp under my feet so if anyone were spying, they would hear me coming, the animals hear me coming, I light up the path with my phone, I can see only one metre in front of me, I don't raise it towards the forest for fear of seeing human-like figures, who am I afraid of, Mum? I'm relieved when I reach the cabin and can let myself in, I light a fire in the wood burner, I light a fire in the fireplace, I don't take off my coat before the thermometer shows 18°C as Mum used to impress upon us whenever we went to Rondane, it is in my blood. It takes less than ten minutes. I am so far away that it can't have happened, yet at the same time it feels as if the worst is over, but it isn't.

Three days later I leave the forest at the same time, but from the opposite side, I get there by ten-thirty and I park in the same spot, except with the car facing the other way, there are many other spots to choose from, but I think of this one as mine now. I don't pay for parking although I'm supposed to. If a traffic warden turns up, I'll drive off. It feels less dramatic than the last time, and indeed nothing happens this time either. I check on 1881 that I'm at the right address, I am, does she spend the whole day indoors? If I stay here till four o'clock, surely I must get a – what would you say, a result? Has she broken her hip? My brain isn't in on this, my brain has abdicated.

I drive home with unfinished business, what is my business? How can I finish it? Life goes by so quickly. There are so many crucial questions we never ask except in our most private moments, so many issues we avoid discussing even though the people who could contribute to clarification and information are still alive. We could seek them out and demand an answer, but we don't, why not? And anyway, we wouldn't get an answer even if we begged and pleaded with them, or it isn't worth the trouble, the humiliation, the awkwardness. We refrain from seeking crucial information to avoid discomfort, and we have but one little life, while the unresolved, the unknown can torment us our whole lives, especially at night, no?

It is possible that Mum doesn't want to talk to me under any circumstances, but I find that hard to believe. Children rejecting their parents is understandable, parents rejecting their children, and with such obduracy, is rare.

I lived in her body for nine months, she gave birth to me in agony and made sure I didn't die, I suckled milk from her breasts, she washed away my body's waste products and dressed me in clean clothes, put me to bed, I presume it was a warm bed. She lulled me to sleep and carried me, even if she did so with very mixed feelings, she cleaned my teeth when I got them, she taught me to speak, ma-ma, in those day mothers alone did that. This person I once believed I was a part of, was symbiotic with, was totally dependent on in every respect, who if she neglected me threatened my very existence, and whom I therefore watched Argus-eyed, my ears pricked, my entire sensory apparatus aimed at her, what did she whisper in my ear back when she lulled me to sleep, *the hand that rocks the cradle rules the world.*

A fresh start wouldn't be possible even if I could make her listen to and somehow acknowledge my story, we're too old for that, but perhaps we could reach a kind of truce. A muting of what I imagine is her constant internal tirade against me, which must be tiresome, also for her; ungrateful, disloyal, attention seeking, heartless.

In the spring before the hot summer I saw *The Wild Duck* at the theatre and it was as if my eyes were opened and I could see clearly for the first time in my life. Being in denial had been hard, but so was facing the truth, how could I live with it? For some people living a lie is essential for them to feel good about themselves, but the lie some people need to live can be the undoing of others, and so I understood Gregers Werle's urge to rip away the veil and open people's eyes so they could see the environment in which they really lived and thus have an opportunity to change their lives. But it takes courage to change your life and there is always a price to pay, and some people have neither the courage, nor are they willing, to pay the price, and nor does it end well in *The Wild Duck*, and so I wanted to protest and cry out when I realised what Hedvig intended to do, he's not worth it, leave now, live your own life! And that same summer I left, but with Mark as my saviour and now that I'm back, am I Hedvig or Gregers Werle?

When did Mum gain a voice and bury my mute Mum whose silent screams I hear all the time?

Every morning I put on my work clothes, open the door to my studio and enter the intoxicating smell of paint, turpentine, dry and wet canvases, but the figure in front of me remains sketchy and uninteresting, the space around it lacks depth. I look at it and lose heart, perhaps coming here was a mistake, 'home', perhaps all the dormant feelings and memories it evokes in me won't inspire my work after all, so is my homecoming proof that I was right to leave in the first place? At the same time I recognise on entering the studio the agitation that usually troubles me just before a breakthrough, only it is so tiresome to have to go through, I draw Mark with charcoal so I have company.

I know the way now and I'm less anxious, less ashamed now, this time I come from the sea and my flat on the thirteenth floor, I sit in the car, contemplating, and today she appears, there is no doubt, why did I ever think I would have doubts, I recognise her immediately: Mum!

Her body is thirty years older, but her posture and gait are still the same, always rushing as if getting somewhere or perhaps getting away from something were a matter of urgency: Mum! Forward-leaning, her gaze alert, her jaw slightly tensed, her steps lighter than I had expected, Mum! She emerges from the stairwell in jeans and trainers, a dark all-weather jacket, but she wears a green bobble hat on her head so I can't see if her hair is still red. She walks the few steps to the pavement, turns away from me and heads in the opposite direction, what had I expected. I make a note of the date and the time.

I usually drive there from the forest, but not every day, the blue-berries have arrived, on the moors I see unripe cloudberries, they stiffen my sinews. I park in the same spot but later in the day, now it's three o'clock in the afternoon. I am no longer on tenterhooks, but I don't read either, I'm in a daze. I recognise the cars I'm parked alongside, three black ones and a small blue electric car, no one unlocks them and drives off, the street is asleep. From time to time a car will pass slowly, a school child with a satchel makes my throat tighten, but then a hesitant car turns up, I slide down in my seat. It searches for a parking space, I turn my face away, it drives past me, I sink down even further, pressing my face against the back of the seat, I know it without knowing it, I feel it, I hear it stop, I hear it parallel park, alter-nately driving back and forth before it comes to a standstill, a door slams, I hear the click as the driver locks it, footsteps cross-ing the street to the pavement, I know it, and I'm right, it's my sister. I look up. Her gait, her body's characteristic movements which live and are scorched into my own, I don't see her face, it is turned away, trained on the entrance to number 22 and wrapped in a scarf, but I see grey hair sticking out at the top, she walks along the pavement slightly pigeon-toed like she used to walk up Blåsutgata to school, her satchel dangling on her back, I didn't know that I could still remember that. She has a handbag slung over her left shoulder and a green Kiwi shopping bag with groceries for Mum in her right hand. My sister walks calmly along the pavement towards the entrance, she is wearing dark trousers, a dark all-weather jacket like Mum's, they look like one another, I wonder if I do? Her walk is calmer and not as rushed as Mum's, she stoops slightly, her eyes on the tarmac. She walks as if she is in no hurry, perhaps she is dreading it, the picture of my sister going to see Mum doesn't excite me, I feel no exhilaration, only a hollow feeling of grief.

She doesn't ring the doorbell, she glances at her watch and lets herself in. There is silence. I see no movements in any of the windows which can tell me on which floor Mum lives, I don't see my sister's figure or shadow in any of the windows which can tell me which flat is Mum's. Shall I stay here until she leaves? I wait forty-five minutes sitting straight up in my seat, suddenly fearless, I wait another fifteen minutes, then another five, but perhaps she is spending the whole evening, the whole night, I drive to the forest although I hadn't planned on doing so, to digest my new grief.

Darkness now falls noticeably earlier, but I'm prepared, I have a torch. I get out of the car and cross the road before I lock it, after the click it gets dark, no stars, no wind and thus no rustling from the trees. For a long time I stand still like a pillar of salt, listening out for any animals though I don't know if their presence would reassure or worry me, I have to get a handle on my new situation. I'm less scared this time although I can see less, my grief pushing my terror aside. My eyes don't adjust to the darkness. The darkness creeps into my pores and fills my whole body, I open my mouth and swallow the darkness, I grow dark from the inside and morph with the darkness and now I see that a path has been created where I have walked because I have taken the exact same route every time, through the low shrubs, through the copse, past the stone that greets me, along the brook, crossing it by the dilapidated old grey cottage with planks of wood nailed across the windows and doors, through yet another copse to the clearing, which opens out despite the darkness, there the cabin waits below a fish-scale moon. My sister's stooping figure, her childhood gait with the satchel on her back, going home to Mum.

I postpone the meeting with the curator. I say my work is going well. It's true in a way.

The blueberries are ripe on the slopes behind the cabin, on the moors higher up are unripe cloudberries, some are already starting to blush faintly, I follow the progress of every single one. I cover the inside of the cabin with reindeer skin and blankets, I get ready to hibernate, I prepare for winter.

I sit in the car, warmly dressed, at a quarter past eleven on Wednesday morning. The entrance to Arne Bruns gate 22 opens, Mum appears. There's no doubt it's Mum. The door closes behind her and she walks the seven metres to the pavement, then she turns right and heads in my direction, she leans slightly forward like Ruth, but with more purpose, her face isn't sad, she strides on resolutely, her legs swift, she is going somewhere. Dark trousers, dark all-weather jacket, a green scarf around her neck, a green bobble hat go with her red hair whose colour I still can't see. A dark brown leather bag over her shoulder, she checks her watch and rounds the corner. I start the car, I reverse in the nearest driveway, I drive down the street and around the corner she has just rounded, there is Mum. I follow at her pace, there are no cars behind me. She rounds the next corner, I follow, Mum can go exactly where she wants to, she turns right, I can't do that, it's a one-way street. I drive as far as I'm allowed, then pull up as close to the pavement as I can, I stop, I get out, I follow the wooden fence to the corner and sneak a peek, Mum is heading for the tram stop, she turns in my direction, looking for the tram, not for me, she doesn't see me, the tram arrives, what is Mum doing? Mum boards the tram and the impotent despair from my childhood washes over me, the contradiction between her obvious suffering and the way she acts as if everything is OK, all the nonsense that used to pour out of her mouth.

Over the next few days I saw four people, two on the moors probably cloudberry hunting and two down among the spruces looking for mushrooms where I had already picked the ground clean. I couldn't relax and drove to the now familiar streets on Sunday afternoon at a quarter past six as it was getting dark. No one was about, it is an area with no shops or cafés, inhabited by old people who prefer somewhere quiet, I have rarely seen a child there. I parked where I usually did and sank into my seat, I didn't leave the radio on because of the faint light it emitted. The wind was blowing fiercely. Leaves fluttered from the maples and aspen onto the windscreen, ginger like Mum's hair, a few fiery red, some were black dots, soon they covered the windscreen and blocked my view, it felt safe. The door to Arne Bruns gate 22 opened and Mum came out unexpectedly, she was wearing a long beige coat I had never seen before, it looked as if it had been bought yesterday, and she had been Saturday shopping with my sister while I was picking mushrooms. Over her shoulder the same brown leather bag, in her hand an off-licence bag with what must be a bottle of wine, she was going out for Sunday dinner with whom? I peered through a gap between the leaves to see her face. She happened to stop below a street light and I saw her face as pale as I remembered it, but not as tormented as I had wished or feared, as if life hadn't hardened her as I had expected or even hoped, but her gaze flitted as I remembered it, she was wondering if she had forgotten anything. She turned decisively, walked the few steps back to the entrance door, unlocked it, entered. I opened the car door and slipped out, closed the door behind me and crept along the fence, past the cars that were parked in front of mine, I squatted down by the rear wheel of the third car, right opposite the entrance. I hoped the owner wouldn't turn up, probably not, the street was asleep, in the few windows which were not already black only the blue glow from televisions could be seen.

Squatting on my haunches for so long in order to avoid being seen was painful, I slipped onto my knees on the wet foliage and felt the moisture seep through my trousers, I leaned on the fender, resting my cheek against the cool, dark grey metal, it smelled like cars did a long time ago. A shadow appeared behind the square windowpanes in the entrance door and moved, Mum came out and looked right at me, I had done something wrong and I was about to be found out. But she didn't notice me, she wasn't thinking about me, what was she thinking about, she had a carrier bag in her hand as well as the off-licence bag, it probably contained a pair of shoes. She went the same way as before, Ruth lived in the opposite direction, seventeen minutes by foot; when she approached the junction, I got up, crossed the street and followed her, she rounded the corner, I rounded the corner not long after her, she wouldn't be turning around, why would she turn around, because of some sudden strong impulse? So I walked with my head down, but without taking my eyes off her, if she turned around, because of some sudden strong impulse, I would bend down and tie my shoe lace except I wasn't wearing shoes with laces, to take a stone out of my shoe then, I had a stone in my shoe, I was a stone in Mum's shoe, but Mum carried on walking as if nothing had happened, she didn't look back, she rounded the corner, continuing onwards towards the tram stop. Several people were waiting for the tram in the twilight with off-licence bags in their hands, they were visiting their families for Sunday dinner, looking forward to it or dreading it. Mum was going to see Ruth, but had decided not to walk in order not to break her hip. The tram arrived, took Mum with it and drove off, I emerged from the shadows and walked back to the entrance to Arne Bruns gate 22 where I studied the names on the entry bell panel, I had forgotten she had a first name. I couldn't work out from the layout which floor she lived on, but I rang Mum's doorbell, I couldn't hear anything and not surprisingly I didn't get a response.

Ruth is waiting for Mum. Ruth hasn't picked Mum up because she is busy in the kitchen making lamb stew and lemon mousse. Ruth's four children are adults and they can drive, but they study at universities outside Oslo. Ruth's husband is away on business. Ruth is expecting Mum. They know each other inside out. Ruth is the person closest to Mum, Ruth knows more about her than anyone else and is most involved in Mum's daily life, in Mum's health. Rigmor also knows about Mum's health, but Rigmor has her hands full looking after her own health, Rigmor doesn't ring Mum every morning and ask her how she slept. And yet I imagine that Mum feels more at ease with Rigmor than with Ruth. Possibly because being with Rigmor isn't associated with duty, because there's no kind of scorekeeping between Mum and Rigmor. I tell myself that there is an account between Ruth and Mum because Mum always knew exactly how much she had given and done, she never forgot any of her sacrifices, she could list them at any time, as she did in her letters to me which were written decades ago admittedly, but even so, amounts in brackets behind many of the entries, presented as if they were evidence of how much she cared while at the same time they hinted at what she expected in return. Mum and Rigmor don't share a trauma. I tell myself that Mum and Ruth can't relax in each other's company, Ruth was never relaxed, I had inherited Mum's lightness, but perhaps Ruth has grown more relaxed over time? Even so I can't imagine that Mum and Ruth can relax when they are together, because their bond is too complex, the past too complicated, it must be exhausting and demanding to mean as much to another person as my Mum does to Ruth and vice versa, but never mind. Mum is on the tram on her way to Ruth's and she gets off at Liabråten, she walks the four minutes to Ruth's house, I have looked it up on 1881, a white detached house, not unlike the one we grew up in. Mum rings the doorbell, Ruth comes to the door and they hug one another. Ruth helps Mum take off the new beige coat, which they probably bought together, and says how nice it is, I think she uses the word *lovely*, it was a good buy. Mum gives her the bottle of wine and Ruth says that she didn't have to. The house smells of lamb stew, Mum likes lamb stew, Mum cooked a good lamb stew, Mum taught Ruth the art of cooking lamb stew, Mum has taught Ruth so many things. Mum takes off her ankle boots and has brought slippers in her carrier bag, she puts them on and enters the kitchen, she knows the way. Ruth studies the wine she has been given and uncorks it because it's better than the one she was going to serve, she says, and Mum is pleased. Mum knows about wine, she learned that from Dad as she did so many other things. Mum asks about Ruth's children even though she is up to speed with them, but young people these days, they're always off travelling or words to that effect. Mum gets a glass of the fine red wine she has brought and settles down on a kitchen chair. She is feeling good now. She slumps in a good way now. Ruth is by the cooker, keeping an eye on the lamb stew, she has made more than the two of them can eat and will freeze the rest. They talk about the guests on *The Lindmo Show*, Mum thinks that one guest, a woman, spouted a lot of silly nonsense, Ruth is used to Mum being scathing about the guests on *The Lindmo Show*, especially the women, but she tends not to contradict her, what's the point. It's not important to Ruth that Mum know what she really thinks about the guests on *The Lindmo Show* or the topics being discussed. I'm quite sure of it. Ruth cares about Mum, but not about Mum understanding her views on complex current affairs, to the extent Ruth has an opinion about complex current affairs, I don't know Ruth. But I'm quite sure that when Ruth and Mum are together that's not what they discuss, they eat and quiet descends, Ruth has made lemon mousse for pudding, Grannie's recipe, our maternal grandmother who died far too young, whom Ruth and I never met. They drink port with the mousse, not coffee, because they are going to bed soon, Mum is staying the night. Ruth has a big house with several bedrooms and she wouldn't let her eighty-five-year-old mother go out in the autumn darkness on streets slippery with red foliage. The hip, always the hip. They sit down in front of the fire.

It's a quarter past ten, I have turned on the patio heater and lit a fire in the outdoor fireplace, I wrap myself in a blanket and look across the fjord. Behind me lies the studio where I haven't worked for a long time, I don't open the door to it so as not to confuse my emotions. If Ruth's house lies in an elevated position, they might be able to see from her windows some of the same things I can see, only from farther away, the fjord itself, but I don't think so. Mum and Ruth look at the fire and Mum has stuck out her feet towards it, Mum gets cold so easily. Ruth goes to the kitchen to clear up the worst of the mess, Mum gazes at the flames. She was told only recently that I live in Oslo now and it came as a shock. They have worked out that

Mark has died. Mina has told someone who has told them. Perhaps Mum feels sorry for me, having lost my husband so early. No, it was worse for her to lose her husband with whom she had lived for many more years and where was I during her time of grief? Mum takes stock in front of the fire. If I had listened to her and Dad and stayed with Thorleif, who, according to 1881, lives in his childhood home with a woman called Merete Sofie Hagen, my life would have looked different and better.

But *if* Mum for a brief moment wonders if I feel all alone in the world, can she share that thought with my sister? That is the next question.

Ruth and Mum have entered into an agreement, possibly a tacit one, about neither of them having any contact with me, a pact Mum can't break. Mum depends on Ruth, she depends on her in every possible way. Mum must act grateful towards Ruth, Mum *is* grateful to Ruth, who meets her every wish, and in return Mum satisfies Ruth's wish not to have any contact with me. If I call, Mum won't pick up the phone. If Mum were to pick up the phone when I called, there might be consequences, Ruth might be offended and pull back and Mum can't risk that. I imagine that Ruth is uncompromising. Ruth probably wonders if Mum thinks more about me than she lets on. Perhaps she is afraid that Mum misses me, the way a wife who has forgiven her husband's infidelity in order to save the marriage continues to wonder if he sometimes dreams about his mistress, *and all that we have lost is ours for evermore.* How frustrating it must be for the loyal, self-sacrificing child if the parents dream about the lost one. I don't think that's the case. I think people who spend time together grow in mutual dependency, that bonds grow stronger even though ties can also constrain and chafe, especially those that are hard to break, they chafe the neck or the ankle where the skin is thin.

Mum sits in front of my sister's fireplace, there are just the two of them in the room. Ruth asks if Mum wants another glass of port as a nightcap, Mum says yes please, what harm can it do. They will be turning in soon, tomorrow is another day, especially for Ruth who is going to work. On her way to work she will drop Mum off at Arne Bruns gate 22, but for now it is a peaceful Sunday in my sister's house, the two of them in front of the fire. Can they open up to one another there, how honest can they be? Can Mum share her innermost thoughts with Ruth, if her innermost thoughts are about me? No. So something remains unsaid between them in front of the fireplace, can't I let them enjoy a little peace in front of the fireplace? But they are most probably in agreement, in harmony, there is total peace in front of the fireplace and good for them.

Do I feel alone in the world? No. Not in the way they think or imagine, because I have always felt alone in the world. It's my default setting. Not even life with Mark could banish it although the feeling lessened during the years I shared with him because he also knew that feeling. Mark, too, felt alone in the world. When he died, I returned to my default setting after the first two years of crazy grief, the feeling of my childhood and youth, it felt almost precious, I had merely had a break from it with Mark. I had my sketchbook, I had my pencils, I have canvases and tubes of paint and brushes, I'm as close to John as I can be to anyone, as close as I dare to be because I'm a damaged child. I don't miss anyone, the only thing I might miss is insight.

I go back inside and happen to catch a glimpse of myself in the mirror and see that my body is morphing into Mum's as if I were clay in a mould.

I end up going to the studio after all and I spend the night there, working with charcoal, not standing up aggressively as I do in front of the canvas, but sitting hunched and closed in on myself over the coarse paper, the sound of charcoal against it calms me. I draw myself as Mum in the mirror and discover that Mum's mouth is doing the talking, it says that she has suffered a great deal because of me.

The next day I wake up late and I pack for the forest, I'm about to drive my usual route, but change my mind, turn right and make my way to Arne Bruns gate. I park in my regular spot, Monday at twelve-thirty. The effort of last night's work still lingers in my hands, they tremble even when I rest them on my lap. The street lies quiet, but why are the trees standing guard? I get out of the car, I cross the street and I hear no sounds other than my own hectic breathing, not the cars farther away, not a tram, I walk around the building with my eyes and ears on high alert, I creep along the wall below the first balcony and onwards under the second, my footsteps are still, the grass and the ground are soft, I round the corner and see an outbuilding with garden furniture, a small playground, some bicycles parked along the wall and three big rubbish bins for recyclables, organic waste and general waste, behind them a green door. It isn't locked, I open it and enter the stairwell, I close the door behind me and listen out, it is as quiet as the grave although I wouldn't know what that's like. I sneak up to the post boxes and I find Mum's among the others, but I can't work out on which floor she lives from its position. There is a lift there, Mum uses it, I take the stairs. I tiptoe, I make no sound, if I meet anyone I'll nod casually, no one will ask me what I'm doing here, a dozen people at least must live in this building, probably more because most people live with someone else, not Mum, not me. I find

125

her name on the third floor, on the door to the right which means that I will be able to see her balcony from the car if I park on the left side of the street twenty metres from the stairwell, if she opens her door now, I'll turn and run downstairs and she won't see me before I'm out of sight. I carry on past her door, up to the fourth floor and onwards to the top floor, I sit down on the stairs there, what am I waiting for? For Mum's door to creak? And then? No creaking, I return to the third floor and I look at Mum's door. She is behind it. Ruth has dropped her off on her way to work, now she is watching nature documentaries from Africa or she is on the phone to Rigmor, I press my ear against the door and listen, but I can't hear anything, I ring the doorbell, then run back up to the top floor, I lie down and peer down the stairwell, Mum's door opens, I don't see it, I hear it, I hear Mum call out a tentative *hello*, but there is no reply. She walks out onto the landing and rests her hands on the banister, I see her hands on the old woodwork, old and wrinkled, but with the same colour nail polish and the ring with the red gem, she looks down, I see her hair, red but with grey roots, I retreat just in case she looks up, I hold my breath, I hear the door being shut, but I can't be sure, perhaps she is trying to trick me, pretending to have given up while what she is really doing is waiting on the doormat. I don't get up, that was strange, a few seconds later I hear her door open again because someone had rung her doorbell, hadn't they, now she is scared that the ringing was all in her mind, that she is starting to get confused, like old people do. I'm sorry, I mumble when she has closed the door again, yet I stay where I am for a while before I get up, just to be on the safe side, which side is that? I don't make my way down until ten, perhaps fifteen, minutes later, I sneak past her door and leave through the green door at the back almost without making a sound. The back garden is deserted, I now know which balcony is Mum's and I leave by going around the other side of the building. My car is parked so that Mum can see it if she leans over the balcony, but why would she? Because someone rang her doorbell a moment ago without there being anyone outside. Mum knows that I'm in town, it came as a shock. I walk in the opposite direction from where my car is, I walk around the block and enter Arne Bruns gate from the other side, I wrap my scarf well around my head, I duck as I walk between the cars and the garden fences until I reach mine, I get in, and I drive off.

I drive to the forest and I arrive in the dark, the crescent moon is green and dangles like a swing in the sky, I light a fire, go to bed and sleep heavily, sinking into myself, not free from fear but still hopeful, because if you have to do something, you should do it as if you meant it. In the morning I drink coffee and go for a long walk to hone in on what it is. Mist rises from the ground and the yellow moors, the crooked pine trees give off a pale glow in the light rain with hoods of grey fog and a smell that reminds me of marrow, the heather glistens and the ferns exude a bitter smell, I greet the wet stone and the tallest pine tree that reaches up to the blue gash in the sky, the wind chatters and pine cones fall, rotten branches snap under my feet and crows gather and caw, I walk down my own path, then follow another, a narrow ribbon with the strangest bends, I walk further and enjoy it; when I get back to the cabin, I soak my thermal underwear overnight and in the morning, I rinse it out three times like Mum taught me, it is in my blood.

The moment I leave the cabin, I feel I'm losing the light, October, early morning, I drive to Arne Bruns gate and I get there around nine, I park so that my car can't be seen from Mum's balcony or Mum's windows, pay for my parking, sling my bag over my shoulder, cross the street and walk along the building opposite Mum's flat, there is a hint of rain in the air. I stop at the corner of the back garden, it lies silent and the trees are on guard, the balcony doors are closed, no windows are open, it's too early and too cold, I cross the garden to reach the cedar hedge bordering the neighbouring building and crawl inside it. I find a suitable spot and set up camp, I spread out my rug and curl up on it. I can't unlock the silence, I have to unlock the silence, I can't attack it, I have to attack it. I belong in these bushes, I can smell childhood and the earth, I have found the best place to hide and no one will ever find me, I hibernate and experience time like someone in the process of leaving this world, behind me time is suspended and I lie homeless in my home, rooted in a state of stagnation. It's Sunday, Sunday.

A memory: When I had painted *There's no place like home* and given it to Mum for her birthday in the morning when we woke her up, so it must have been in the autumn, perhaps around this time and Ruth wasn't there, I think, so it must have been in Year One, Mum said, once Dad had gone to the office and I was about to walk to school, she opened the front door for me and I stepped outside and she bent down and whispered in my ear: My special girl.

Later she said it at least three times when no one else was listening, when I had drawn something she liked, my special girl, then she stopped, when and why I don't know, but she never said it again.

The green door squeaks, it is heavy and it opens slowly, out steps an old man with a Kiwi shopping bag in his hand, he goes to the general waste bin, he struggles to lift up the lid, then slings the bag over the edge, I hear it hit the bottom as if the bin is empty. He goes back in the way he came out. I curl up inside the cedars and see everything with unreal clarity. The tiny droplets of rain on the green blades of grass, a glimpse of the sky between dark, waxy leaves when I lean back my head, a ray of autumn sunshine on something that sparkles in the ground: a treasure. I reach out my hand and dig out a metal Tuborg bottle top, it is old and possibly valuable, it certainly brings luck. I squeeze it in my hand and remember something in a hot glimpse, then the door squeaks and the memory slips away like my night-time dreams returning to the vault where I create them, Mum appears with a Co-op bag in her hand. She isn't wearing a coat, she has just nipped down to take out the rubbish, dark trousers, a grey rolled-neck lamb's wool jumper, her hair put up in a bun like before, she goes to the general waste bin. She holds the bag in her left hand and is about to lift the lid with her right, but it is heavy and she can't lift it high enough to get the bag over the edge, she stands on her toes, but her arm isn't strong enough, she sets down the bag in order to lift the lid with both hands, she takes hold, lifts it, rises up on her toes, the lid trembles, Mum's arms tremble, she stretches further and then further still, gives it a push and lets it go, the lid wobbles for a few quivering seconds before it falls open, she did it! She slings the bag triumphantly over the edge with a defiant swing and leaves without closing the lid.

I let it sink in, I close my eyes in order to digest it, I hibernate and I lose sense of time, I sink into myself and down through the ground to everything that is buried there, the green door opens and a young man comes out, he goes over to the bicycles, unlocks a modern mountain bike and pushes it away, I roll up my rug and return it to the bag, calmly I step out of the bushes and walk to the bin without fear, I've accidentally thrown out something I didn't mean to. I almost upend it and look at the bags, there is only one from the Co-op, I pick it up and pull the bin upright, I close the lid, I leave the way I came and decide to drive to the flat. Twenty minutes later I let myself in and go to my studio. The Co-op bag doesn't smell of rubbish, I tip out the contents on my worktable and wonder if I'm getting closer now or just farther away. There is a cloudburst, the sky falls onto the skylight in the studio, over the loo roll and the plastic bag empty of dried apricots which, strictly speaking, should have been put in the bin for recyclables, eggshell and onion peel, which should be with the other organic waste, an empty tin of chopped tomatoes, packaging from 250 grams of mince and the kitchen table comes back as do the café curtains with the yellow flowers, homework and the smell of fried onions and the boiling saucepan with spaghetti, Mum fishes out a strand of spaghetti with a fork and chucks it at the tiled splashback behind the cooker, if it falls down, it means it isn't ready, if it sticks, it's al dente and fine. Two burned-out tea lights, a full vacuum cleaner bag and underneath it a broken Chinese porcelain cup, oh the terror. I was eleven years old and home alone, that was very rare, Mum was always at home, but not that day, I don't know why, perhaps she had gone shopping with Rigmor. Home alone and the living room was quiet, only the big antique cupboard whispered. It contained Dad's evening tipple, and chocolate. From the big windows I could see the drive and the road, when Mum came back, I would know well in advance. I fetched a stool from the kitchen so I wouldn't have to reach up on my toes, I didn't want to act with impatience or in haste, but savour it. I climbed onto the stool and opened the door to the forbidden crystal glass bowl with the pale pink, lilac and white Anthon Berg Opera mints, they hadn't counted them, surely? I popped a pink one into my mouth in order not to torment myself any longer, the road was still clear. If Mum had appeared in the bend, she wouldn't be able to reach the garden gate until I had finished the mint, I could swallow it in one single gulp, I closed my eyes to keep out any distracting sensory impressions. I sucked off the crisp sugar shell, then the chocolate, then the mint fondant, I made it last as long as I could, I swayed faintly on the stool and came round when the mint was gone though the strong taste lingered in my mouth long afterwards, the road still lay empty. On the shelf below the bowl with the mints, was the Chinese tea service Dad had inherited from his grandparents in Bergen, it was only ever used at Christmas and on Constitution Day when the adults would drink coffee from it; the delicate teapot decorated with dragons and women with big flowers in their hair was never used. Resting on top of the porcelain was a box of chocolates, I lifted it out, opened the lid and saw that there were exactly so many pieces left that it would be difficult to know that one was missing unless they had counted them, I took the chance, I picked one with a caramel centre, put the lid back on the box, returned it, closed my eyes and concentrated. I bit off the chocolate bottom with my front teeth, then sucked out the filling as slowly as I could, I licked caramel off the chocolate shell with tiny flicks of my tongue, my mouth burned from sweetness, I swayed with pleasure and I lost my balance, I grabbed hold of the cupboard for stability, but my hand brushed against a cup which fell and smashed against the floor, I woke up with yesterday's world in pieces between the legs of the stool, suddenly cold. The drive was still empty, the long road sunny and sleepy as if nothing had happened, I prayed that Mum would never come home. I ran to the kitchen with the stool, found the dustpan and brush, ran back, looked out of the windows, no one in sight, picked up the larger shards with my hands, swept up the smaller with my heart pounding in my throat, I couldn't just chuck them in the bin, I found an empty bread bag, tipped the shards into it, tied a knot on it, ran to my room and hid it under my duvet, ran back to the windows, the drive was still empty, I counted the cups in the cupboard, twelve, so there had been thirteen, I took the thirteenth saucer, ran to my room and put it in the bread bag under my duvet. I don't remember us ever being thirteen at the table, but perhaps we would be thirteen for my confirmation in four years, if it wasn't discovered before, it would be then. It was a long time to dread. But it might be discovered sooner, as early as tomorrow, even today, at any moment today, I had to be vigilant every single minute. Mum would occasionally invite friends home and though they rarely numbered more than four, it wouldn't surprise me if Mum counted the cups before she set the table in order to calm herself down, the way I counted things to calm myself down, the steps to the bridge across the big road, twenty-one, the steps from the ground floor to the first floor, fourteen, in order to keep my world spinning on its axis; what you count over and over stays in your head in contrast to chocolates and mints whose numbers are constantly changing. The drive was empty. No one except me could have broken it, Ruth was too young. But might Ruth be a suspect in three years? No, it was me who broke cups, broke hearts, I had accidentally broken Mum's mirror-backed hairbrush and she said that I had broken her heart, I was the one who got on people's nerves. You get on my nerves, Dad said, your mind is twisted, Dad said. My home-work was to draw our house, we had all been told to draw a picture of the place where we lived, I sat at the kitchen table and I had finished drawing our house and I had written *our house* underneath it when Mum came in, looked over my shoulder, then she gasped for air, it was as if the winter and the mute darkness outside the windows in which I saw Mum's face reflected had taken up residence in her eyes as I stared up at them in terror, and Dad came in, suddenly he was standing behind me, I could see him in the window against the winter darkness, bigger than I had seen him before, as big as a spruce tree, Mum took a step to the side, Dad picked up the sheet of paper, looked at it and asked what it meant, the darkness outside forced itself into my head and into my mouth, I swallowed the darkness. Is that supposed to be our house, Dad said. Is that what our house looks like, Dad said, and I realised that I would have to leave home immediately, except I didn't have anywhere to go. Your mind is twisted, Dad said, scrunching up the sheet of paper and then he left, that's how I remember it. Mum picked up the paper, threw it out and told me to go to bed, she would come to my room once I was in bed. I washed my hands and face as I had been told, as if in a trance, I cleaned my teeth, got changed and lay down under my duvet, Mum came in and sat down on the side of my bed, switched on the bedside lamp and said: You can draw the house now if you do it quickly. That way you can hand in your homework tomorrow. She fetched my sketchpad and my box of colouring pencils, placed them in my lap, I sat up in bed, she sat down again. You know that our house is yellow, Mum said, passing me the yellow pencil, I drew the house Mum and Dad thought they lived in, yellow with white windowsills and a white door and café curtains with yellow flowers in the kitchen window, the apple tree, said Mum, and I drew the apple tree while Mum followed my hand, the gooseberry bush, Mum said, I drew the gooseberry bush with its unripe gooseberries, and noticed that Mum's eyes had shifted from my hand to the floor as if she were studying a particular knot in the wood, and she looked miserable, I drew a kitten in the porch and I was done. Mum jerked as if she had woken up from a sad dream and put on a front, let's have a look, she said, I gave her the drawing and she looked pleased, she pointed to the cat and asked what it was. A cat, I said, we don't have a cat, Mum said, but perhaps one day we might get one, I said, I would like a cat. Mum said that if I drew a cat, the teacher might think that we had one and that would be lying, I said the cat could be visiting us, she passed me the rubber and I erased the cat. Done, Mum said, turned off the light and left.

I rearranged the cups so that anyone opening the cupboard wouldn't notice that one of them was missing, so that there wasn't a gap left by the broken cup, which would otherwise *leap* to Dad's eyes when he went to get his Saturday brandy. There was still no one in the drive. I went down to the hall and outside, I stood in the porch, closed my eyes, then I opened them imagining I was Mum and entered the house, still imagining I was Mum, tossed Mum's bag onto the chair the way she always did, walked up the stairs like Mum, smoothed my hair like Mum always did, and felt like Mum, we became one, I looked across the living room imagining I was Mum, and Mum's eyes landed on the cupboard, but the cupboard seemed innocuous and there were no traces of any crime on the floor, then I saw Mum walking down the road, but she was slow because she was holding Ruth by the hand. I ran to my room and found the bag under my duvet. It was a Tuesday and my bed linen wouldn't be changed until Sunday, I stuffed the bag in between the slats and the mattress, I sat on the bed and I heard the saucer break, I jumped up and down a couple of times and I thought I could hear the fragments being ground to flour, tonight I would take it out, hide it at the bottom of my satchel and chuck it in the bin by the bus stop on my way to school. If contrary to her usual habit Mum were to perch on the side of my bed tonight, something she didn't normally do, would she notice the bag? I smoothed my bedspread and sat on the bed imagining I was Mum and felt nothing, but Mum was probably like The Princess and The Pea. I couldn't think of a better hiding place before the door opened downstairs. I put my satchel on the bed, took out my Norwegian book and sat down at my desk, they came up the stairs still slowly because Mum was guiding Ruth. Mum called out my name, I replied I was doing my homework. They went into the kitchen to unpack their shopping, after some time I joined them and said I was going to the tennis court to watch the players. She asked how my geography test had gone, that was why I had come home early because I had done well in my geography test and finished early, I knew all the Norwegian towns from Kristiansand to Hammerfest in the right order. Great! I said, and Mum asked if I could list the towns from Kristiansand to Hammerfest in the right order for her, and I could, and Ruth sat under the kitchen table watching me with her mouth hanging open, they were impressed, as I remember it, my mind wasn't twisted, come here, Mum said, I was her special girl, she plaited my hair with loving fingers, I had inherited Mum's hair, the fire from Hamar.

That evening when Mum came to say good night like she always did, when she would stand in the doorway and say: good night, Johanna, like a rhyme that didn't rhyme before she closed the door, on the day of the Chinese porcelain cup, she entered my room and a chill went down my spine, she had noticed its absence and would have to tell Dad who was watching television in the living room. She stood by the side of my bed, dreading it, I wanted her to put me out of my misery and just tell me right away, then she perched on the side of my bed without knowing she was sitting on the missing cup ground to powder. I remember the day we were told that Uncle Håkon had died. Mum had sat down on the side of my bed and asked if I was upset and I didn't know what to reply, I tilted my head to one side and tried to look sad. It's just the way life is, Mum said, then she left, I remember her words even though there was nothing original about them. But on the day of the Chinese porcelain cup, she also came in and sat on the side of my bed and the cup didn't make a sound, but that might be because the blood was frozen in my ears, the door was open behind her and the small lamp on the chest of drawers in the passage was still lit, it wasn't normally, she usually turned it off before she opened the door to my room to say good night, Johanna, she was looking for the thirteenth cup, she was sitting on the remains of it as she said and I remember every single word even

139

though there was nothing special about them. *Today, on my way home from town, I saw a big yellow bird*. I didn't know what she wanted me to say. She scrutinised me, then said as if it might be a question that it couldn't have been a budgie because it was too big for that. I still didn't say anything, she sat still for what felt like a long time, then she said, oh well, got up and left.

Back then I didn't understand the significance. Mum didn't trust her own senses, Mum doubted what she saw and couldn't share it with Dad because Dad would say that her mind was twisted. If Mum had told Dad that she had seen a big yellow bird, Dad would have said that Mum was mad, bad, that rhymes. Mum told me about the bird on the day the thirteenth cup got broken.

Only eleven Chinese porcelain cups remain in Mum's cupboard now unless other cups have been broken since I broke the thirteenth, perhaps Mum breaks Chinese porcelain cups on a regular basis, they all belong to her now, I imagine her hurling them onto the floor with great force, a liberating sight, Mum swearing like a sailor, Mum is clearing out the closet, but who is she raging against, me? Mum has done a thorough job with the dustpan and broom, all the pieces are here; with the help of a magnifying visor and a pair of tweezers I glue them back together, I paint the splices with liquid gold leaf, I name it *Yellow Bird.*

Some inclement days followed. The fog drifted across the fjord and settled on the ships so only their funnels could be seen, it muffled all sounds, including theirs. I longed for the sky and wanted to go to higher ground to see it, but still I drove to Arne Bruns gate and parked in my usual spot, which happened to be free, I waited fifteen minutes. As always the street lay quiet, Saturday morning, grey, glum, chilly, but wasn't that my sister's car parked on the right-hand side of the street further ahead of me, or did I only think so because it was red. The door to Mum's stairwell opened and Ruth appeared. She held open the door for the person behind her, Mum. Ruth took Mum's arm and they slowly walked to the pavement, they turned in unison in my direction, they knew where they were going, they approached me, without knowing it, one step at a time, Ruth with her head bent towards Mum, she was much taller than her, taller than me, Mum looked smaller arm in arm with Ruth, Ruth was chatting. Gauging from Mum's facial expression, it looked as if Ruth was issuing orders, but I'm no impartial observer. Arm in arm with Ruth, Mum looked as if she couldn't walk without holding someone's, my sister's, arm, a strange sight, where were they going?

They passed my car without knowing I was in it, they wandered down the street, oblivious to me, didn't sense my presence although I felt so very present, Ruth and Mum, arm in arm down the pavement as if nothing had happened while I sent them burning thoughts, they turned right at the junction, to hell with paying for parking I thought and got out, they knew I was in the country, but it would never occur to them that I might be nearby, they had managed to remove me so far from their hearts and minds, I followed them at a distance of thirty metres, it was cold and so there was nothing strange about me wrapping myself in a scarf, they themselves were wrapped in scarves, Ruth in a grey one, Mum in a green, down the street towards what, mother and daughter arm in arm, one a younger version of the other, like me, a variation on a theme, in dark all-weather jackets, Mum's dark green, my sister's dark grey, with practical black ankle boots with low heels, Mum wearing a green bobble hat, always green because she has red hair, as do I. My sister didn't wear a hat, my sister has grey hair, my sister carries a rucksack, what's inside it, arm in arm down a street I haven't walked before and whose name I don't know, I'm the prodigal daughter who has come home, but there is no one to welcome me, it's my own fault. I came back to seek and she who seeks shall find, but not what she is looking for. They turn at the next junction and I realise it: they are going to the cemetery, they are visiting Dad's grave.

The worst remains, but the long mental journey is behind me. Dad is dead and I thought Mum was dead in me, why would I resurrect her, is that what I'm trying to do? Whenever I wanted to be happy, I had to forget Mum and Dad. I had to tell my heart to calm down behind my ribs, don't tire yourself out like that, heart! Soon I'll be going home to my true mother, the forest where I have made my nest.

Ruth and Mum, arm in arm thirty-five metres ahead of me like two grieving figures in harmony, how long is it since Dad died? They walk as if Dad died yesterday, they walk as if they are grieving, but they are not grieving me, they need a pure grief and have created a pure grief for themselves, they visit Dad's grave every Saturday morning whatever the weather, it is a ritual which confirms and consolidates the pact on which they both depend, but in different ways, they have entered into this pact for different reasons, but they never talk about that, the terms and conditions of the pact, but what do I know. Dad died, but his death didn't set Mum free nor did she want to be free, she didn't dare, she had always been under his guardianship and she let herself be treated as a minor now, she depended on my sister, and couldn't separate from her, and loved her, of course, I see what I want to see. There is rain in the air, the sky is heavy, its heaviness sags right down to the ground and the trees at the cemetery look poor, stripped of their leaves, the branches spiky against the fog, helpless and glum like burned fingers, Mum and Ruth trudge between the gravestones as if they had just received the sad news that Dad is dead, they need this ritual of grief, it makes them feel something, but what? A sense of belonging, a shared history, it was like that, wasn't it, yes, it was.

The cemetery is almost deserted, a few similar figures stand or walk near its edges, stooping slightly, grieving, or so they look to me. They know where they are going, my sister and Mum, my gaze probably flits more than theirs even though I'm hyper-focused. It feels milder the further in we get, the closer the big trees stand whose delicate top branches the fog prevents us from seeing. The raw birch trunks give off warmth and there are tall bushes with wine-red leaves that stay wine-red all winter, and in between them old, venerable graves partly overgrown with moss, some with tall columns and statues, Head Clerk Fredrik Holst lies to my right, is this where Dad is buried? I've never thought about Dad having a grave, I didn't attend his funeral, for me the story ended there, but now I wonder if perhaps that is strange and unnatural, perhaps it's shameful that I have never spent a moment wondering where Dad is buried, has lain buried for all these years, where is Dad's grave? And that's another reason they don't want to have any contact with me, because I haven't shown any interest in Dad's grave. But I'm here now.

They don't talk now, they look right ahead, their bodies radiate concentration, they approach their destination, they walk slightly faster, they round a corner by a bench, I stop at the bush behind it, I can just about see over it that they have stopped by a relatively new stone, I watch it and them from the side.

Ruth has taken off her rucksack and squatted down, she clears away leaves and dead flowers, she has taken off her mittens, she brushes away pine needles that have fallen from the surrounding trees, a scrap of paper and a burned-out grave candle; she bends over her rucksack and takes out a small wreath of moss and heather, not a round one, not heart-shaped, it looks like a big tie pin, it is because we are by Dad's grave. Mum stands motionless, her gaze on the stone, what is Mum thinking? Ruth unpacks a grave candle, she doesn't look at Mum, Ruth is used to Mum standing like this when they visit Dad's grave, Mum stands as if petrified. I catch myself wanting Mum to speak sharply to Dad at last. Ruth lights the candle, places it in front of the headstone, she rearranges the wreath so that it lies nicely placed in relation to the candle, looks at her work, brushes leaves and soil off her hands, picks up her mittens, but she doesn't put them on, she glances at Mum, Mum stands still, from the side it looks as if she has closed her eyes. I remember the one time I saw Mum going up against Dad, it was during the special girl period, and I felt myself seen, we were alone in the kitchen, Mum was by the cooker, I was at the table, drawing. She liked my drawing, she encouraged me to draw, she had been the best at drawing herself when she was at school, she had told me, and she taught me how to draw roses, one leaf after another going from the outside and in, and she said with an expression in her eyes I interpreted as jokey: Can you draw Grannie Margrethe?

She went to stand behind me, bent down and I felt her plait brush my neck like a caress. I drew Grannie Margrethe's sharp centre parting, her stern eyes, the large brooch on her chest and finally her mouth with the downturned corners, then Dad came in and Mum jumped and Dad saw the drawing and his look darkened and Mum paled and had nothing to do with it, have you no respect, Dad said, snatched the paper and tore it up, I went to my room, I heard Dad talking before it grew quiet and I imagined that Mum loosened up her hair and became fully Dad's, but perhaps I make that part up because I need to.

Ruth glances at Mum, she seems to heave a sigh, then she breathes in and out quickly as if reacting to some kind of disappointment. Ruth packs up her rucksack, she has done this many times, once a week for fourteen years with Mum and knows where to dispose of the burned-out grave candle, the weeds and the waste, it is less than a metre away from me and I hear it fall into the bin, if only you knew that your special girl is crouched behind a bush, watching you. Ruth rejoins Mum and stands next to her, they linger for a few seconds, Ruth puts her arm around Mum's shoulder and Mum seems to wake up and then slump, she shakes her head, and says so that I, too, can hear it, Ah well.

Please let me see your eyes! Your big dark eyes! They are cold, yes, I know! But let me see them, let me look deep into them to see if deep inside them there might be a thought for me, a small good thought about me!

The fog descends and it starts to rain. Ruth takes off her rucksack and finds a folding umbrella, she has thought of everything. She unfurls it, Mum steps under it and they move even closer and more slowly, and raindrops the size of grapes explode against my head and run down and under the lining around my throat and neck, Ruth and Mum don't go back the way they came, they walk around the big tree by the boulder and the fog comes down like a low ceiling. Ruth and Mum disappear under the black, slightly swaying umbrella and look like a ghost, they look like Death in an Ingmar Bergman film, a clumsy and awkward, crooked and weary Death and for that reason all the more frightening, I don't follow that Death. I sit down on the ground with my back against the bush and feel the moisture seep through my trousers and underwear just like when I was a child. I sit in the rain at the cemetery where he is buried, and pick at the soil for a fragment of a bathroom tile, preferably a blue one, while the rain slams down, bucketing, it is heavier than normal rain and the sky is greyer than it usually is when it rains.

When I turned twelve, I got a 50-kroner note in the post from Grannie Margrethe, who would occasionally pay us regal visits from Bergen and make the fire from Hamar blush. Dad told me to put it in my piggy bank, but I didn't. The next day there was a teacher training day at my school and Mum had a doctor's appointment and had to take me with her and afterwards we stopped by the bookshop because Mum needed to buy stationery, she wrote regularly to Uncle Håkon and Aunt Ågot in Hamar. The bookshop had a section with drawing materials, and I fell in love with a box of one hundred and fifty different colouring pencils, costing 49.50 kroner, I had my 50 kroner note with me. Mum said what Dad invariably said whenever we wanted to spend money rather than save it: A fool and his money are soon parted. But I had turned twelve and I reminded myself that I was twelve now and repeated to Mum what Grannie Margrethe from Bergen had said when she called, as she did on every birthday, that I could spend the money on anything I wanted, it wasn't true, but it really was. It was liberating somehow not to be the special girl anymore, no matter how wonderful it had been while it lasted. I bought the colouring pencils. As we left, Mum repeated: A fool and his money are soon parted.

When I drew, I got away from myself or maybe I got away from Mum.

When I draw, I get away from myself or maybe I get away from Mum.

I walk along the road below the cabin and notice a stone in my shoe. I leave it be. I have a stone in the forest, it lies at the end of the path where the mound opens out and it is smooth and broad, at times I lie down on it to rest, but as I walk on, I can still feel the stone in my shoe, that's Mum.

I text John: Everything OK your end?

That's all, I wait until Sunday, good boundaries are important.

Once I was thirteen years old. I came home from school and the table was laid in the dining room, my parents had guests coming the following day, no more than eight fortunately, important guests, rich, Mum said with fearful agitation, I thought it was very grand that my parents knew rich and important people. Some small white cards with gilded edges had been laid out on the kitchen table, place cards on which I was to write the names of the guests and draw some leaves. She said it as a straightforward order, as if she had told me to make my bed and tidy my room, but the implication behind it warmed my heart: Mum thinks I write neater letters and draw finer leaves than she does, I felt very honoured and loved Mum. I fetched the box with the one hundred and fifty colouring pencils and thought that now she would regret saying that bit about a fool and his money. She had written the names of the guests on a piece of paper in capitals and I was to copy them out in joined-up handwriting. Two of the names were American, they were the rich ones, if they agreed to work with Dad, we would get rich too, it was an important dinner and very important place cards. Mum made lemon mousse, there was a pot of lemon balm on the windowsill, I was to draw lemon balm leaves in the corners of the cards. I picked up the turquoise pencil, but she wanted me to write the names in red. I said that turquoise was nicer if I were to draw the lemon balm leaves in the colour they have in real life, but I could also make them pink. Pink? she said, sounding flummoxed, but lemon balm leaves are green, she said, picking up the pot from the window and placing it in front of me, don't you see, yes, I said, but you want the names in red? Mum looked at me with uncertainty, paused for a moment and then she said, I'm in charge, it's my dinner party. We both know Dad's the one in charge, I said, thirteen years old and rebellious. Have you no respect, she said in a harsh voice, have you no respect for your mother, she said sharply, sounding like Dad, I wrote the names in red, in joined-up writing. And lemon balm leaves in the corners, she said in a softer voice, I drew a lemon balm leaf in the corner, it doesn't look like one, she said, yes, I said, no, she said, look, she said, snipping a leaf off the plant and placing it in front of me, I drew the lemon balm leaves like Mum wanted them, then I got up. Do you want a chocolate biscuit, she said, I shook my head. No? No, I don't want one, I said, something had been stuck in my throat, it felt good to get it out.

No, I don't, no, I don't want, Mum said, you're so negative. It's hard to love people who are negative. Princess-no-I-don't, Mum said, it doesn't end well for her.

One Christmas Grannie Margrethe Hauk from Bergen gave me 100 kroner. Ruth got 50 kroner because she was younger, but she would soon grow old enough. When we visited the Christmas market over the holidays and stopped at the wood-carver's stall, I wanted to buy a chisel, and Mum heaved a sigh: A fool and his money are soon parted.

It echoes in my ears now as it did back then, but something happened before that.

I came home early from school one day, we had had a test and I knew all the answers because I was special, I rushed home to be alone with Mum before she had to pick up Ruth, I ran up the stairs and saw Mum standing on a chair in front of the large antique wall cupboard, she was holding the Chinese porcelain vase she and Dad had been given as a wedding present by Grannie Margrethe, Hi, I said, Mum turned, saw me and dropped the vase, or so it looked to me, it fell onto the floor and smashed. We both froze, Mum on the chair, me on the top step, the fourteenth, it was unbelievable, the most valuable object in the house, Dad's pride, and Queen Margrethe's stake in our lives.

Mum on the chair, me with a white hand on the banister, the world silent, the world had never been more silent, my blood drained like molten lead from my heart to my feet, my brain howled with sirens from police cars, fire engines and ambulances.

Mum climbed down from her chair, walked with what I remember as controlled steps out into the kitchen, returned with a dustpan and brush and said: I don't think Dad will be very happy. Mum swept up the pieces and threw them in the bin, there was no point in trying to hide something that would inevitably be noticed and have consequences, it was only a matter of time and punishment.

I had been beaten twice before, I don't remember what for, breaking something, talking back, you'll get a beating when your Dad gets home. Mum hadn't said so this time, but it was in the air, I had never caused anything worse than this. I lay on my bed and waited, Mum picked Ruth up, I'm guessing she cooked dinner, Dad parked the car, Dad opened the garden gate, Dad walked up the garden path without me hearing his footsteps, the front door opened, Dad came up, Mum didn't go down to meet him as she usually did, I had harboured a wild hope that she might come to my rescue, I realised now that wasn't going to happen, Dad entered the kitchen. Mum told him about the vase in a voice so low that I couldn't hear her words, but she couldn't say that I had smashed it on purpose, what did Mum say? Dad swore, Dad said *damn* and suddenly appeared in my room and ordered me to stand up, I wasn't even halfway up before he grabbed my chin with his hand, bent down over me and shouted: Do you understand what you have done? His accent became broad just like Grannie Margrethe's and with that grimace his mouth took on whenever she visited, a mixture of rage and terror.

It was my fault. I had rushed up and distracted Mum, startled Mum, Dad would never know nor would he ever understand that the offence had taken much longer, that was something only Mum and I knew, except that Mum didn't want to know or remember it. Mum had stood holding the vase, she must have heard the front door open and close, she must have heard my footsteps on the stairs because she turned to me with a gaze that said she had been expecting me, she fixed my gaze for some seconds before she let go, a deliberate act, I see it now like a slow-motion movie retrieved from the void of oblivion. I had never forgotten this incident, such incidents can't be forgotten, but I had stored it in my brain's chamber for shame and crime, and now I replayed the film and proved Mum's complicity. But then again, I had known it at the time, I *saw* it.

I understood only too well why Mum would want to smash that vase. I, too, would have wanted to smash it, especially if I had been Mum which in a way I was. Mum was brave enough to smash it, I'll give her that, finally an appropriate response, a run-up to a protest, but Mum wasn't brave enough to see it through and afterwards she hated me for having seen both her desire and her cowardice.

Dad screamed at me, Mum didn't come in, and still I didn't give up hope?

I had repressed the incident in order to go on hoping, what else had I forgotten for that same reason?

I called Pax to ask if he had had a frank conversation with his mother before she died. He said there hadn't been anything to talk about. He hadn't felt the need and didn't think his mother had either; he had visited her many times in the days before she passed, they both knew that she was on her deathbed, and yet there had been silence between them, but not one that was uncomfortable. It grew silent between us, but it wasn't uncomfortable; after a while he said that he hadn't realised how definitive it was. He hadn't truly understood until long after her death that she was never coming back, that he would never hear her voice again. Never. Even on her deathbed, he hadn't understood what it meant. Had he understood it, he said, he might have, he broke off. You might have what, I said, might have what? Thanked her, he said.

I was reminded of that movie by Roy Andersson where a toy salesman sits in a depressing hotel room and plays a record of the song 'Pretty Little Anna If You Will, Listen to Me with Your Heart and Soul', over and over, especially the final verse *and together we will go to heaven, where we will see Mum and Dad again,* as the tears roll down his cheeks. His colleague enters and is taken aback: Why are you crying? Because I won't get to see my Mum and Dad in heaven.

Once I was fourteen years old. I had stopped eating that year. I saw a movie about a girl my own age from a middle-class family in an English suburb, the only child of parents who fretted about their reputation. The young girl had a wild streak which I recognised, but the friend with whom I had gone to see the picture wanted us to leave, nothing's happening, she said, but I couldn't take my eyes off the girl on the screen whose parents didn't understand, but sensed and feared her wild streak and took her to the doctor because she must be ill. When she didn't do what they wanted and talked back, the doctor agreed that there had to be something wrong with the girl who turned her back on them and didn't answer their questions and showed no *respect*, and he wrote a prescription for pills for her, which she refused to take and she managed to trick her parents, but eventually they found out and her Dad was furious and wanted to pin her down so her Mum could stuff the pills down her throat, but the girl spat them out and wiggled free and ran out of the door and her Dad called the psychiatric emergency ward and they agreed a plan because when the daughter came home later that night having run screaming around the English moors like Judith Shakespeare in A *Room of One's Own*, the psychiatric paramedics picked her up by force and drove her to a remote, castle-like building intended for such girls, and when her parents picked her up a year later, she was fixed and took her pills without any protests, true, she looked totally uninterested in herself and the world, but she took her pills, so it was a kind of happy ending.

I stopped eating that year and anything I did eat, I threw up as if the food Mum cooked might change my personality, might be pills that would dampen my wildness, I had grazes on my knuckles from the shameful vomiting and my weight dropped by twenty-five kilos, Dad didn't notice anything, of course, but how could Mum not? I'm glad I saw that movie, I didn't want to be unprepared, I stopped eating that year, I practised self-discipline.

Doesn't Mum remember? Doesn't Mum ever look back?

She must stick with her chosen strategy. Mum has opted for the role of the betrayed mother. Her daughter has publicly dishonoured her by exhibiting paintings with seemingly neutral titles, *Child and Mother 1* and 2, but neither the child nor the mother in them look happy. However, this is the worst: The daughter didn't come to her father's funeral.

That's what she's like.

But at night when she lies down to sleep? What does she think then, what kind of conversation does Mum have with herself? Does Mum consult her deepest self?

Do I consult my deepest self?

I didn't go to Dad's funeral because I couldn't. I preached the gospel of everyday life. I had always struggled with religious holidays, parties, the rituals that Mum cultivated, dressed up for, dressed up as, life is a stage and all that, except the domestic one didn't count as far as Mum was concerned, everyday life within the four walls of our house and my intense gaze didn't count. Mute and jealous, I would watch her in front of the mirror, Mum excited because she and Dad were going to a party or were hosting a party. I didn't go to Dad's funeral because I imagined Mum in black, the grieving widow, Mum's face adopting the expression of her role, and I knew the role I had been allocated, the ungrateful daughter, disloyal, and I wouldn't be able to escape it because everyone else was sticking to the script. I didn't travel home to Dad's funeral because I wouldn't have been able to cope, and when I arranged Mark's several years later, it was as simple as it could be, just John and me, a couple of colleagues, the gospel of everyday life and all that. I did it for John, so he wouldn't feel awkward and pressured, I told myself at the time, but I guess it was mostly for my own sake. I consulted my inner mother and did the opposite of what she would have done.

I have often wondered what Mum would say, if contrary to expectation she were to see a psychologist. But she won't. She hasn't changed that much.

Mum's strategy requires her to pull herself together, for Mum to hold her head up high, but does she ever lie down and curl up?

Mum taught me to draw roses, thank you, you start from the outside and work your way in, thank you, Mum was also good at drawing when she was little, but the leaves on the roses I drew started to wither and drop off and then I stopped drawing roses, then I stopped showing Mum what I had drawn because I knew pretty much what she would say: Your obsession with ugliness is childish. Only little children think it's brave to say fart and poo.

I stuck to my plan and drove to the forest even though I was soaked through, I expected the sky to be blue higher up. Twenty kilometres from the city the rain stopped, two kilometres up the steep Kolleveien I saw blue sky and it hadn't rained when I parked, the road was dry. Halfway along the path, the sun came out and the morning I had spent in town belonged to a former life. I lit a fire in the wood burner and in the brick fireplace, peeled off my wet clothes, changed into dry ones, closed and locked the cabin door and walked across the meadow to the deep pool where the river bends, but not so far that I couldn't see smoke from my own chimney. The moss was still lush and green, the foliage on the alder bushes dense and dark, the shallow water in the brook trickled and filtered reassuringly over the golden stones and the light foam around them glittered in the sunshine, the air was cool. The uniform, undulating darkness of the big spruce forest lay behind me like a warm wall and in front of me like a promise, as tranquil as if it was fast asleep and I thought I could feel how the sap rose slowly in the trees and in everything else that grew, heather and brushwood and a belated bluebell in between the blades of grass, they were preparing for the frost. And it felt as if life also stirred, sleepy and silent, inside my body, as if my grief settled in me and fell asleep.

Once I was twenty-four and newly married. I was reading Law as my Dad had wanted me to and therefore Mum did too, and I was more removed from myself than when I was fourteen and starving myself, I had encapsulated my rage because I was scared of what it might do if I didn't, I guess I had learned that from Mum.

It was summer, I was on a train to Arendal, Thorleif's father's sixtieth birthday it must have been, Thorleif had gone on ahead to help. Mum and Dad would arrive by car the next day, on the day of the birthday.

I had chosen an empty compartment in order to study, I had brought books, the dreadfully heavy *Laws of Norway*, I read it diligently that summer to get it over with, it was an unbearable course, I wanted to shorten my suffering. A woman entered, sat down opposite me and gazed calmly out of the window. Her hands rested calmly in her lap, she exuded serenity, she couldn't be much older than me, but so calm, I didn't think I had ever met a woman so serene. Her presence lit up the compartment or it grew lighter outside, there were rolling fields of wheat now and occasional clusters of trees with small sparkling blue lakes surrounding small green islands, she smiled. I tried to carry on reading, but my eyes kept straying to the landscape outside and when I looked at it, I couldn't avoid also looking at

172

her, she was wearing a summer dress, her blonde hair fell loosely over her shoulders and she was smiling. Just as my eyes had left my book yet again, she opened her bag on the adjacent seat, took out a miniature bottle of champagne of the kind they serve on planes, was she going to drink it now? She went to the door, opened it and looked outside in both directions, then she winked at me and said that the coast was clear as if we were playing a game. She removed the metal wire from the bottle-neck and twisted the cork, there was a quiet plop, I'm celebrating, she said, I've landed my dream job, she said, as a gardener at the Lunde Museum, I'm so happy!

I didn't reply, what could I say, Cheers, she said, and I looked up and she explained that she had just finished a horticultural course at Vea College; her parents had said she would never get a job as anything other than a nursery gardener, but now she would be responsible for eight hundred and twenty trees, two oaks and ten flowerbeds at the Lunde Museum, isn't that amazing, I nodded. What do parents know, she said.

It grew quiet, her words lingered in the air, then she asked what I was studying in a voice so calm that I couldn't reply in my own which was rough and cracked, I raised the book so she could see the title, she nodded and I lowered it, she asked if I wanted to become a lawyer or join the police force and arrest people like her who broke the rules by drinking alcohol on trains, I stared hard at the pages where the letters merged into one another, I felt a lump in my throat and my shame made me wish that the earth would swallow me, I'm just joking, she said, leaned towards me and brushed my knee, where are you going, she asked in order to save me.

I, I said in a trembling voice, my husband and I, I said and

173

blushed, but I couldn't call him my boyfriend because we were married, newlyweds, because my husband's father, I said, my father-in-law, I gulped, it's his birthday, she suggested, yes, I said, she nodded towards the book in my lap, are you excited about graduating?

Excited? I must have looked astonished and she felt the need to explain. I'm *excited*, she said, and I looked at her and wondered if I had ever felt excited about anything as a grown-up, but if I had got my dream job, especially one my parents didn't think I would get, then perhaps I would have felt excited? The thought immediately made me feel heretical.

Nordagutu was announced on the speaker system and that was her station, she said, drained the bottle and put it in the bin, now people will think you drank it, she said, only joking, she said and the train stopped, she got off, and walked across the platform with swift but calm footsteps, which were excited, and disappeared into the summer, the train continued, everything continues, *what do parents know*. I saw Dad as he had been at my recently celebrated wedding, the stately and natural host, my mother as she had been at my recently celebrated wedding, the hostess with the mostest, her finger on every detail from beginning to end, it hadn't been my wedding, I realised, not even Thorleif's though he probably told himself so, I had felt alien and remote from start to finish and had gripped the seat of my chair so hard when Dad made his speech that when he was finally done, I couldn't pick up the cutlery to eat the saddle of reindeer, arty-farty academy was still ringing in my ears; then I remembered what Mum had said when she called me this morning to tell me not to wear the blue floral dress I had worn for Ruth's birthday, it was too shabby, Dad had been embarrassed, I had so many nice skirts and white blouses and so I had packed a grey skirt and a white blouse and Thorleif's bowtie, which he had forgotten, and that was a disaster and so on, I had done it without thinking like a robot in motion, but what did I want? I got off the train in Arendal and walked through the underpass towards the town centre and the seafront, Thorleif hadn't arrived yet. I went to a telephone booth and entered the number for home, through the glass windows I could see the marina and Thorleif when he turned up. Dad answered, I said that I had arrived, that I would like to talk to Mum, I had hoped he wouldn't be at home, I was already losing heart, Mum came to the phone and asked what I wanted, that was a good question. I braced myself and said, and it sounded like a question, that I had thought I might apply to the Arts and Crafts Academy in the autumn. Mum didn't reply, but the silence that followed spoke volumes, and yet it got worse when she opened her mouth. *The Arts and Crafts Academy,* she echoed as if it was the most ridiculous idea she had ever heard. Are you going to spend the rest of your life throwing pottery? The kind of tat they sell from craft stalls, which no one ever buys. There's no money in it. I didn't reply. *Johanna,* she said again with a sigh as if I was five years old, I was five years old, and Thorleif arrived on the boat, wearing a blue captain's cap, well, you'll have to take out a student loan, Mum said, and it's *your* life, she said, but it wasn't. What's the point of remembering moments that can't be changed? Mum rang off and I walked towards my newly minted husband, I didn't mention the conversation to him, and when Mum and Dad arrived in their car the next day, they said nothing about it, either, Mum never mentioned it, it was as if it had never happened, and that was to spare my blushes, I guess, she didn't want to remind me of my foolishness, my childish whim, in order not to embarrass me, how could I ever have hoped for Mum's support, why had I even called her in the first place, but then again it would later turn out that I had a habit of calling Mum when I shouldn't.

But it has all burned itself out of me.

Some days the things that don't happen are the most important ones. I called Mum, she didn't pick up. The year has sixteen months. November, December, January, February, March, April, May, June, July, August, September, October, November, November, November, November.

My sister doesn't know what happens to the relationship between mother and daughter when the daughter doesn't want to live the life prescribed for her, but to live her own life. When the mother fights the daughter, and the daughter fights her own fearful self, the two of them tied together by pain and rage, and it becomes a matter of intimacy, not love. Such intimacy is merciless and merciless intimacy is erotic and will destroy one of them. My sister knows nothing about that, she hasn't inherited Mum's red hair, my sister is no fire from Hamar. Growing up makes no difference.

I remember a picture of Mum and me, a small black and white photograph from when I was a baby, I carry it in my heart, it's in a cigar box somewhere, I smile and Mum smiles and there is no one else in the picture and Mum is happy and focused on me and life can't get any better, Mum is young and pretty, and it's just the two of us.

The evenings grow shorter. From my hideaway I watch the last leaves fall, the dwarf birches blush, the moss turn grey and the grass lie down to sleep when darkness falls, insects die or hibernate, everything waiting for winter, for iron nights. A solitary cloudberry quivers in the shadow of the big spruces where memories wait, the hand trembles in November. Branches breathe in the darkness and the moors drink up the vast night, there is whistling and creaking and I cling to this exhausted life as if it were a treasure.

The door opens to Arne Bruns gate 22 and Mum appears. She isn't meeting my sister, she isn't meeting Rigmor, she is out on her own and I'm excited, where is Mum going? Sunday morning at ten o'clock, it's misty and there is sleet, it's sleeting, the snow melts on the tarmac and turns into slush, Mum walks doggedly through the slush, eagerly almost, where is Mum going with her head held high, what's Mum doing?

Mum turns right and continues up Arne Bruns gate, away from me, she has gone that way before, she walks with purpose as if she is out on an errand she has chosen for herself and not told anyone about, what is it? A date? Then she would have walked differently, or would she? People over eighty go online and find someone they can enjoy their final years with, especially those who have spent a lifetime with another person, someone who has suddenly died, people who aren't used to being alone, who miss company, it's not necessarily about love. That might be true of Mum, no, I don't think so. Or don't I want to think so? Mum has Ruth and Ruth's family and that's enough for Mum, but what do I know? It's early Sunday morning. Mum turns right at the junction, I turn right at the junction, she isn't going to turn around, given her determined stride, I follow at Mum's pace thirty metres behind her, ready to bend down to remove a stone from my shoe, the sleet keeps falling, it melts on my nose and upper lip, it lingers on my eyelashes before it melts and turns into droplets on my cheek which remind me of . . . then the memory is gone. Mum crosses the street, I cross the street, Mum turns left onto the pavement, I turn left onto the pavement, I gain on Mum and try to be as strongly present as I can, to send Mum vibrations of my presence, but they don't reach her, she carries on regardless, seemingly unaffected by me, while a young woman, who comes towards her and passes her, notices my presence as if it slams into her chest, she gives me a startled look and swerves around me, I carry on regardless, I gain on Mum, I'm less than ten metres behind her, but Mum doesn't sense me, her mind is on other things, she is finally out on her own, surely I can allow her that, she walks with purpose towards what? She is fast for a woman of her age, carefree for a woman of her age, I walk carefree at Mum's pace, I copy Mum. She approaches the lights and the main road, the light glows green for pedestrians, Mum marches on, the light turns amber, Mum doesn't slow down, it turns red, Mum doesn't slow down, Mum hasn't noticed the lights changing or her eyesight is bad or she thinks she can make it across before the cars start to move, but they are starting to move and Mum walks on, I run up to grab her when she suddenly stops as if she was just trying to trick me, I stand close behind her on trembling legs and the smell of my childhood wafts towards me in the cold air, her old-fashioned perfume mixing with the smell of white rolls and almond oil, I retreat, overwhelmed by bygone feelings, images flickering before my eyes, I memorise them for later contemplation, like a monk, I hold my breath, I take another step back, I bump into a man, I slip around him and stand behind him until the light changes to green. Mum crosses the pedestrian crossing, I follow on amber, I hear church bells in the distance. There are several people on this pavement, more bodies to hide behind,

Mum walks with the same determination and speed past the slower ones, men with sticks and shrunken women, there are more people the closer we get to the church, surely she's not going there? At the junction she turns left down Kirkeveien, as if she is going to church, Mum walks through the church gate and up to the main entrance, I don't believe it, do I follow her there?

It can't be a wedding because I would have been able to see that, it can't be a christening either because I would have been able to see that too, it's an ordinary service and Mum is going to attend it? We never went to church. At Christmas, of course, but then again everyone did, it had nothing to do with religion, it was about tradition, just as mandatory as roast pork, we never went to church on Sundays. It might be a carol service, I decide, to calm myself down, Mum has reached the steps, a concert to celebrate advent, I think, to calm myself down, why do I need calming down? Because I'm hurt by the enormity of the change of heart which Mum must have undergone if she now considers herself to be a Christian without me knowing about it or being a part of it. I'm hurt by the notion of the seriousness Mum must have felt in that respect without me having any idea about it. Why? Because I had yearned for seriousness in Mum! I had never thought of Mum as a serious person. Had Mum become a serious person in my absence? Had I hurt Mum so much that she needed religion to comfort her? No, because if she had turned into a deeply serious person, she would have picked up the phone when I called. Anything else was impossible. Mum couldn't simultaneously be very serious and at the same time not want to have any contact with me! It was impossible! Mum? The half-averted figure exaggerated to mythical proportions who had dominated my childhood and my youth, had she been converted to something as all-embracing and serious as the

Christian faith and still she didn't want to see me? It was a harsh punishment.

Mum walks up the steps to the church as do other similarly winter-clad advent figures, most of them old women, men die, women are widowed and they are going to church because there is a carol service, that must be what it is. No one there is under forty. Mum enters and I follow, I stop in the porch to see where she sits down. There are no signs of a concert, no instruments, no technical equipment, no one takes any notice of me standing in the porch, scanning the church. The few people who come in are preoccupied with the steps, relieved to have managed them, growing ever more anxious the older they get, frightened they won't be able to do the things they need to do, the doctor's appointment, the train, the church service, they loosen their scarfs, take off their hats, mittens, stuff them in their pockets and bags, Mum stands inside the church, still wearing her bobble hat, She is the only person to take a seat on the ninth pew to the right below the pulpit, an exposed place, she can't hide from the vicar there. Most people sit near the front in order to hear better, twelve people in total, ten women, two men, I'm the final person to enter and the thirteenth at the table, I'm Gregers Werle with his demand for the ideal, Mum takes off her green bobble hat and her hair is red and held in place as it was for all those years I remember it, with a broad tin clip at the back of her head, Mum, Mum. I walk along the wall to the left and pick the eighth pew where a woman already sits near the centre aisle, she blocks my view of Mum, she covers me, but if I lean forwards or tilt back my head, I hope I'll be able to see Mum's face. I don't take off my scarf, I sink into the scarf, I have a cold. I count the tousled backs of people's heads, old people forget to brush

184

the back of their head or they can't reach with the comb, but Mum's hair has been styled as always, it might be dyed but it is still red. She waits in anticipation, in contrast to the others who slump out of habit, Mum is excited, why? The vicar arrives dressed in white with a rope tied around his waist, he is in his fifties and devoid of charisma, she can't be there for him? He says what vicars say, words and phrases from morning prayers at school, white noise in the background. The Lord bless thee, and keep thee, the Lord make his face shine upon thee, and be gracious unto thee blah-blah. Organ music flows from the organ loft and changes everything, it grows warm, I don't know the hymn, no one sings, I move forwards, I watch Mum. Her lips don't move, she is pale but composed, her face unusually open, hungry almost, in a way I haven't seen it before, but then again it's so long since I last saw it. The vicar prays, the vicar prays for the sins of the congregation to be forgiven, mine included, a soporific mumbling, the vicar steps into the pulpit, the congregation lift their faces towards him, he leans forwards and talks about the beginning of sorrows, in a flat soft voice. *And ye shall hear of wars and rumours of war; see that ye be not troubled: for all these things must come to pass, but the end is not yet. And there shall be famines, and pestilences, and earthquakes, in diverse places. All these are the beginning of sorrows.* The woman next to me is asleep, Mum hangs on his every word. *But beware of men: for they will deliver you up to the councils, and they will scourge you in their synagogues. And brother shall deliver up the brother to death, and the father the child: and the children shall rise up against their parents, and cause them to be put to death,* in an undramatic and neutral voice. *But he that endureth to the end, shall be saved.* Mum's brown eyes are fixed on the vicar's slightly forward-leaning, sleepy figure, I don't understand it.

When ye therefore shall see the abomination of desolation, Then let them which be in Judea flee into the mountains; Let him which is on the housetop not come down to take anything out of his house: Neither let him which is in the field return back to take his clothes. Pray that it doesn't happen in winter! Winter is coming, the church pew is cold, the cold penetrates my clothes and my skin, goes into my spine, then up into my head where it settles over my brain like a helmet. *For then shall be great tribulation, such as was not since the beginning of the world to this time, no, nor ever shall be.* The vicar turns the page, turns to the wrong page, he has to leaf back, he finds his glasses, finds his place and carries on while outside the sleet lashes the stained-glass windows:

The sun shall be darkened
and the moon shall not give her light
The stars shall fall
from heaven
and the powers of the heavens shall be shaken.

And they shall see the Son of man coming in the clouds with power and great glory. Yet again I look at Mum, Mum is crying, tears flow from Mum's eyes, it's incredible, Mum is crying. Elizabeth was old and had given up on having a child, but an angel from the Lord came to Zechariah and said that Elizabeth would bear him a son and his name would be John, Mum cries. Zechariah couldn't believe it because he was so old and Elizabeth was old, too, but the angel replied that he was Gabriel, who represented the face of God and that Zechariah would be struck mute because he didn't believe it, and Zechariah was struck mute, but Elizabeth got pregnant and gave birth to a son, and everyone thought he should be named Zechariah after his father, but Elizabeth said that his name would be John, Mum cries. People said no one in their family was called John and gestured to the father, Zechariah, to find out what he thought the child should be called, he asked for a tablet and wrote: His name is John. And everyone was amazed, but at that moment Zechariah's mouth was opened, and his tongue loosened, and he started to praise God. Mum's narrow shoulders shake, Mum's pathetic figure shakes and I finally understand: She goes to church to cry.

I'm not allowed to see what I have seen. I have trespassed, I'm the unwelcome, unwanted thirteenth guest at the table for whom there isn't a Chinese porcelain cup, and yet I don't leave because suffering is a link which brings a magical pleasure happiness can never deliver. I grip the pew hard, bow my head, close my ears, shut out the noises in the church, make it dark behind my cold forehead, I start to count and it works. I don't know for how long, but suddenly I hear the organ, 'Abide with Me'. It's evening time, it's advent time, winter is coming, night is coming, and no other help will do. I hug myself and lean forwards, Mum cries, oh, you helper of the helpless, Mum's eyes brim over and *swift to its close ebbs out life's little day, fast falls the eventide; the darkness deepens, earth's joys grow dim,* Mum raises her hand and wipes away her tears, my throat stings, I fight it, *Change and decay in all around I see; O Thou who changest not, abide with me, O Thou who changest not, abide with me.*

People start to get up, the woman next to me has stood up and is moving slowly towards the aisle, Mum stays where she is, opens her bag, takes out a handkerchief, briskly dries her face, then puts it back, she arches her back as she gets up, shaking herself loose with a shrug of her shoulder, which reminds me of something, but then it is gone. Mum raises her head and leaves with the same determination with which she entered, I stay put. The verger comes over and asks if I want a word with the vicar who is still in the sacristy, I shake my head and get up, I go to the porch, it's empty, no one is waiting. It won't take Mum long to walk home, her green bobble hat pulled well down. I imagine her in Arne Bruns gate, it's time to stop.

Outside the grey sky sags down to the street which is black, shiny and covered in rotting leaves, it is dark and people wear dark clothing to merge with the darkness and not be seen, they have dark rings under their eyes and dark hearts underneath their clothes. My car stands dark among other dark cars, I get in and turn on the ignition, the dashboard lights up, ah well. I drive conscientiously, I signal in every roundabout, stick to the speed limit, follow the signs *slavishly*, it takes concentration, soon I reach higher ground. At the top of Kolleveien white snow falls, higher up the snow begins to settle, white, further up it is like a fluffy, warm duvet that softens everything sharp. I arrive, the road has been cleared, but the path is snowed over, I sink into the snow up to my knees, I sink into it up to my hips, my bag is heavy, I consider leaving half its contents behind and making two trips like a polar explorer, but conclude it won't save me any time and I have no need to save time, I waddle on in the snow and my mind can rest, I find a rhythm, I'm a fat duck. I don't cross the meadow, but walk alongside it at the edge of the forest where the spruces grow so close that no snow can fall between them, where the earth can breathe, I circle in on the log cabin and with every step I see it from a new angle, I don't cross the snow until the distance is at its shortest, thirty metres at most, I approach it from the rear, I set down my bag on the stone threshold and clear the snow with my feet, there that's done it. I light a fire in the wood burner, I light a fire in the brick fireplace, I open the bottle of red wine which hasn't grown cold. I sit on the kitchen stool while I wait for Mum's 18°C, I look at the meadow which has no footprints, it glitters in the faint yellow light from my windows, the moon hangs in the sky like an upended soup bowl. Sunday 1 December, it's ten o'clock, I call Mum, she doesn't pick up.

December, advent calendar. Every morning I would open one door and I would be excited about it because that was the whole point. Behind it would be a yellow plastic figure, a sheep or a shepherd. Behind door number twenty-one would be a yellow plastic ring, I looked forward to it, but I had to wait until the twenty-first; I had sneaked an illegal peek and thought the ring must be some kind of reward because what did a ring have to do with the baby Jesus? Ruth had the room next to mine, how Ruth felt about the advent calendar and the yellow plastic sheep I don't know. On Christmas Eve it would be Mary with the baby Jesus, I knew that because I had already looked although I wasn't supposed to. I never expected there to be anything more exciting behind the doors when I opened them, whether or not I was allowed to look. The advent calendar was accompanied by a fear that my peeking would be found out. Did Ruth sneak a peek? What do I know? Mornings were dark and cold, days short and sad, the trees stood black, the scruffy bushes sagged, the garden fences slumped despondently, the garden gate squeaked on its hinges, the few birds that hadn't migrated or fled tweeted wistfully, but one morning when I pulled up the blind, the world was bright and new, pure snow had fallen, the sky's cool white sheet had been spread across berry bushes and cast iron gates, even the big apple tree was covered in snow.

The night is iron blue and iron grey, but by morning more snow has fallen, the world is white and a rift appears in the present, a hole opens up in time, it was a Sunday and we were going out. Every Sunday we would go walking or skiing when it was skiing weather as it was now on this particular Sunday. Dad and Mum and Ruth and I were going to ski from Vassbuseter to Trovann, but on this particular Sunday Mum was ill. I was in bed, Ruth and I were still in our beds as we tended to be on Sunday mornings while Mum and Dad sat in the kitchen, drinking coffee. The aroma of coffee filled the house and everyone's movements were slower than on weekday mornings; as always I lay with my door ajar and my ears pricked up, Mum said, I'm not feeling very well. I reached out my hand and pushed open the door a little farther, straining to hear, Mum said, It started last night, I'm not feeling very well, it's my head, you know, and I ache all over. That was something to remember, *It's my head, you know, and I ache all over.* I had had a nightmare the night before and gone to them in the living room hoping that Mum would walk me back to my room as she sometimes did when I came to see them after a nightmare, but she just said, Go back to bed, Johanna. And yet I had lingered in the hope that she might walk me back after all and tuck my duvet around me so her red hair, which was loose in the evenings when Dad was home, would tickle my face and it would smell of almonds because she

193

had her own special shampoo which thickened her hair and made it shinier, and which I would sometimes steal and then be terrified that she would smell the theft on my hair. Go back to bed, she said, and I went back to bed, but from my bed, I heard Dad say, *Not her again.* Dad speaking like that had made Mum's head hurt and her body ache all over.

If we knew, if we understood when we were young how crucial childhood is, no one would ever dare have children.

Mum could get sick like everybody else. Dad couldn't insist on Mum skiing from Vassbuseter to Trovann with a headache. The moment I heard that Mum was sick, I got sick and my body started to ache all over. I lay under my blue gingham duvet, so that's why the blue gingham duvet cover has survived every move, I realised, Mum coughed, I coughed, Dad got up and went out into the passage, opened Ruth's door, said, Ruth? He didn't wait for a reply, he opened my door and said, Johanna? He didn't wait for a reply, but told us both to get up and get dressed because we were going to Vassbuseter and then to Trovann. I coughed and said that my head hurt as did my whole body. Dad came in, turned on the light, went to the window and pulled up the blind, the sunlight poured in, there's some bug going around, I said. Dad left, went to the kitchen and told Mum that I had *said* that I was ill. I imagined Mum slumping in her chair, she had been looking forward to having the whole day to herself and now I had ruined it by being ill. Dad asked if she thought we should all stay at home, cancel the trip, but Mum said no no, no no, she insisted that Dad go skiing in a voice which wasn't sick. I lay as quiet as a mouse. Mum got up, her chair creaked, soon she appeared in the doorway, Dad *says* you're ill? My head hurts and my body feels funny, I said, it'll pass, I said. She made no reply. I think it's best that I stay under the duvet and lie very still all day, I said, so that she would

196

understand that I wouldn't bother her. I simultaneously hoped and feared that she would place her hand on my forehead to feel if it was hot and discover that it wasn't, but she didn't, she just left.

I didn't feel safe until they had gone. Ruth was up and dressed, Mum made them breakfast even though she was ill, she made them a packed lunch and a flask of cocoa which Dad packed in his bag, I heard everything, finally they all went down to the hall, the front door opened and I thought I could feel the cold winter air, I heard Mum say, Have a nice trip, I heard Dad reply, We will, and I thought he was glad that I was ill. Because when Mum was ill, then I was ill and then he could ski from Vass-buseter to Trovann with just Ruth. The front door closed, I waited for Mum, she didn't come. She tidied up clothes, she wanted to be alone, she wanted this bright winter Sunday morning all to herself. She had seen a forecast yesterday and made a plan, but then things hadn't gone according to her plan because I felt ill. And maybe she suspected me of pretending to be ill when I wasn't just to ruin things, that thought couldn't be thought, I dropped the thought. Mum thought I was ill and I had to make sure she continued to believe that and lie limp and mute under my duvet all day. But why did I get ill when Mum got ill, if I was just going to lie mute under my duvet all day, what was the point of my illness, I don't know. I heard Mum walk up the stairs with heavy footsteps because I was in my room depriving her of the joy she had been looking forward to.

I decided to lie as quiet as a mouse in the hope that Mum would enjoy her alone day so much that she might start to miss being with someone, me, for instance, I closed my eyes in order to hear better. She went to the master bedroom and got into bed. I hadn't expected that. She wanted to get some more sleep. I tried to get some more sleep, but I couldn't, I could hear my bed linen rustle whenever I breathed, I stopped breathing in order not to hear it, I pushed the duvet down to my hips so it wouldn't move when I breathed, then I heard a kind of buzzing in my head, I bumped it against the wall to make it stop, that worked, it grew warm behind my eyes in a good way, then I heard animals inside the wall and snow falling from the branches of the apple tree outside, Mum was asleep. Or maybe Mum couldn't sleep because of me, like I couldn't sleep because of her? I needed the loo, but didn't want to go to the loo for fear of waking Mum if she really was able to sleep in spite of me. I don't know how much time passed before I heard Mum's door open and Mum's tentative footsteps in the passage. Mum savoured the Sunday silence and her solitude and tried to forget that I was around, perhaps she succeeded. I wanted and yet at the same time I didn't want her to succeed. Mum went to the bathroom and closed the door; if she had been on her own, she wouldn't have closed the door, she would have peed with the door open, something she had been looking forward to, but now she couldn't because of me. So she had some awareness of my presence; that was good. Mum flushed the loo, left the bathroom and went to the kitchen. The sound of the tap, she was making coffee and then she would join me. The water stopped running, the coffee was brewing, Mum didn't join me. The coffee was ready, I could smell coffee, the aroma of coffee suppresses fear, Mum didn't come. She poured coffee into the green cup with the gilded rim, how green was my childhood's mother. She opened the cupboard, I heard a rustling of cellophane, she was going to have a chocolate biscuit with her coffee because it was Sunday and she had forgotten that I was there. Mum sat in Dad's chair and looked out at the white fields and the birch trees with their white trunks on the margins, the apple tree by the gate whose branches were so high that I could reach them from my window. Mum's body ached all over. She sat in Dad's chair as she looked out at the landscape she was limited to, couldn't escape, two children and a husband which it was her job to take care of, Mum stared at the ground with empty eyes: Who would have thought that my life would turn out like this! I was overcome with compassion for Mum which I desperately wanted to express, I had an urge to run out and hug and comfort Mum, to thank her for staying though she would so obviously rather leave. But I reckon it was my own impossibility I projected onto Mum back then, today I think it was about my own desire to escape, something I didn't dare acknowledge at the time because I was even more trapped in the square yellow house than Mum. So maybe I was wrong, perhaps Mum was contented, perhaps Mum sat in the kitchen deeply happy, looking across something she thought of as familiar and loved, that is to say, she would have been completely happy if it hadn't been for her older daughter lying sick in the room next door. How was Mum? I wanted to run out and put my arms around her in the hope that she would welcome me and lean her sad face against mine and say, my girl, so that we could be sad together rather than separately. I didn't do it, I didn't dare go to the loo because I'd risk seeing disappointment in Mum's brown eyes at the sight of me, an unmanageable, exhausting caretaking responsibility from which she wanted to be released. Mum fetched a second chocolate biscuit and I couldn't hold it in any longer, I slipped out of bed as quietly as I could and tiptoed to the bathroom, Mum didn't hear me or she didn't

199

want to hear me; as I had imagined she was sitting in Dad's chair with her back to me and the rest of the rooms, facing the earth and the trees, I closed the door, I put loo paper in the bowl to muffle the sound, but I couldn't muffle the sound of flushing when I had finished, it rumbled and roared, then it went quiet, I listened out for Mum, I opened the door carefully and saw her sitting as before, motionless, her face turned towards the window, I tiptoed back to my bed, my heart pounding. Perhaps Mum really was mortally ill. Yet again I wanted to rush out and fling my arms around her, yet again I didn't. If Mum died, I would die, too, there was no doubt about it. A chill spread from my forehead to my shoulders when I heard Mum's footsteps in the passage, my heart jumped to my throat and I struggled to breathe, I pressed my eyes shut. She appeared in the doorway, I detected Mum's night-time smell from her dressing gown. So you're ill, she said, I nodded. She grew quiet, she wondered what to say next, as did I. What would she have done if I hadn't been here, if it hadn't been for me?

She said, Are you well enough to eat breakfast in the kitchen? What was the right answer? My guess was that she wanted to eat breakfast alone. I replied that I thought it best to stay in my room and she left. It sounded like she poured more coffee into the green cup with the gilded rim and sat in Dad's chair, I wondered if I had given the wrong reply. She pulled out a drawer and opened a kitchen cupboard, I lay with my eyes shut and listened to the sound of running water, a saucepan on the stove, a knife against a plate and footsteps in my direction, she nudged open the door with her foot, entered with a tray and asked me to sit up, placed the tray on my lap and said, You can be a princess now, then she left. On the tray was a boiled egg, a salt shaker, a knife, a teaspoon, a plate with two slices of bread, one with goat's cheese, one with jam, a glass of milk and a paper napkin with gold stars from Christmas.

I listened out for her, I couldn't hear anything, was she sitting in the kitchen listening out for me? How much food does a sick person eat, I wondered? Whenever one of us caught a cold, Mum would mix egg yolk with cream and juice oranges for us because a sick person needs nourishment to recover, I decided to eat the egg. I cut off the top, but aimed too low, the yolk spilled over the egg cup and onto the napkin, which couldn't be saved, I licked off as much of the yolk as I could and ate the rest of the egg, I wiped up the spillage with the napkin, folding it into a square and pushing it into the empty shell, drank a little milk, then I waited.

Footsteps in the passage and Mum in the doorway, going by her face it looked as if I had eaten the right amount, she removed the tray and returned with her silver brush, perched on the side of my bed and asked if I wanted to brush her hair. I had used her silver brush in secret and she knew it, I couldn't lift it. She turned to me quizzically, I picked it up anyway, pressed it carefully against her head and pulled it down also carefully, lifted it, pressed it carefully against her hair, dragged it down also carefully, you're not doing it right, she said, I didn't dare do it any harder, the brush was too heavy, I really did ache all over, Mum heaved a sigh, took the brush from me and left, she returned it to the chest of drawers below the mirror in the master bedroom where it usually lived, came back and told me to get up and put on my dressing gown, she waited while I did it, then asked me to join her in the kitchen, she took out the family art box, pulled a chair out onto the floor, sat down on it and asked me to draw her, she must be very ill.

I knew how to draw. You would have to give me that. Dad didn't like drawing, we have cameras now, was Dad's response when Mum said she had been good at drawing flowers when she was little, he gave Mum a camera as a birthday present, she never used it, but when I had drawn some bumblebees for my biology homework and Mum showed them to Dad, he said, The girl knows how to draw, I'll give her that. I sat down at the table and started flicking through the pages of my sketchpad. Whenever I couldn't sleep at night, I would pretend that Mum had been kidnapped by robbers, but if I was able to draw her so that they knew who she was, they would let her go, I was allowed only three colours, I chose black, red, brown. I outlined Mum's heart-shaped face and Mum's eyes with black, I drew large ellipsis-shaped pupils in her brown eyes, her mouth as a red heart in her heart-shaped face, finally her hair loose like the robbers liked it, first in red then brown on top and Mum was released and grateful that I had saved her, and I could fall asleep, I drew Mum in my sleep.

I asked how many colours I could use, as many as you like, her expression was one of challenge, narrow, squinting eyes and a wry smile on her lips which I failed to interpret, I was suspended in the air, the goalkeeper's fear at a penalty shootout.

What did Mum want? Was she wondering how I truly saw her? It was a tantalising thought. I picked up the brown pencil and drew her narrow eyes, I had to be honest and true. Our teacher said that the Second World War could have been avoided if people had been honest and true to their hearts despite threats of punishment, *reprisals*. I understood what he meant, I picked up the red pencil and drew her mouth which said, Have you no respect for your mother? Spoken like an accusation but with the grammar of a question because I didn't respect her in the way she wanted me to. My mind knew too much without knowing it, but my hands knew, I drew Mum's red hair loose for Dad, which Dad sniffed with his eyes closed, Dad liked Mum's hair, but he didn't respect Mum or Hamar where she had grown up, perhaps without being respected as an equal member of the family, I painted the smallholding in the background, Mum wanted the respect from me she hadn't got from others, she couldn't see it herself, she had blind spots, I drew them, I drew what I sensed, what I vaguely felt, she asked if I was nearly done, I drew a thought bubble over her head, only the hands remained, I let her have them in her pockets.

Mum paled. The fire from Hamar had been extinguished. Mum raised the sheet to her face and overcame an impulse to scrunch it up, it was what she had suspected, I had been honest and true.

She put it down on the cooker, but the rings were turned off. She asked if I thought she should show it to Dad, I shook my head. She asked if she should frame it and hang it in the living room. I shook my head. She said I could put it in the cigar box I kept under my bed. The blood rose to my face, she knew about the box, had she opened it? She walked past me out of the kitchen to the master bedroom and closed the door, from here there was no way out. I had written in code, but had she cracked it? Then I must die. If I had been able to feel my legs, I would have run outside and jumped into the river, then she suddenly appeared in front of me with her hands behind her back: Left or right?

What was she doing? She fixed me with her eyes, I raised a numb hand towards her left and she held out her hand, there was a tin box in it, I looked up, she nodded vehemently and I took it with considerable apprehension. Open it, she said, and I opened it, it contained pieces of torn paper. That's me, she said, pointing to the tin box, fetched the drawing from the cooker, pointed to it and said: That's you! Put them both in your cigar box and find a better place to hide it, she said and gestured for me to leave, I took the tin and the drawing back to my room and sat on my bed, she must be very ill.

She ran a bath, I waited until I heard her get into it, then I crawled under my bed, fetched the cigar box and opened it with Mum's eyes. It wasn't as terrible as I had feared. Many of the drawings were of her, but they were drawn for the robbers, there was a notebook with encoded writing, she couldn't have cracked the code, I no longer remembered it myself, then a small page written in normal writing, but it didn't say that Mum was bad, a five-øre coin I had found in the street, which brought luck. I put the tin box and the drawing in the cigar box and put it back under the bed, got into bed where I lay rigid like a stick, visualising square blocks which I counted as I slid them from one side of my forehead to the other, I had got to three hundred and eighty-four when I heard the car, I went to the window and saw them get out. They looked normal, as if everything was normal. Dad took down the skis from the roof rack and put them in the garage, Ruth waited, then he took her hand and together they walked up to the house, they didn't look up at my window, as if everything was normal. I got back into bed and listened out for Mum. She, too, had heard the car, she opened the door to them and was well again. We were having spaghetti for supper though it was a Sunday because she had been ill and apple crumble for pudding because that, too, was easy to make as long as you had all the ingredients. I heard Mum cook the spaghetti while Ruth sat under the table like in a novel, Mum took a single strand of spaghetti from the saucepan and threw it at the tiled splashback behind the cooker, it was ready. I ate dinner at the table with them, I, too, was well, infected by Mum and would be going to school the next morning, it was as if this morning never happened. Mum did the ironing for the rest of that evening.

The winter cold has arrived and with it sleeting rain, I look at the leaden fjord and ask myself: What am I doing here? The ridges look back at me with cold eyes, I'm no more at home here than anywhere else, what am I doing here? She who has run away, will never find her way home again, why don't I go somewhere I have never been and hide there? I go to the cabin on the barren ground and close the door, but the wind roars and buffets, the rain teems down and batters the roof, my thoughts spin and I writhe because I am alone. My heart aches, it trembles and flits, trapped behind my ribs. I made myself homeless and homeless I am, and my anguish will not be stilled. Hailstones lash the window and teeth gnaw at the walls, steel knuckles bang on doors, paws maul, creatures sigh, wanting to get in, the terror arrives, the great darkness rises from the forest and the sky hangs low over me like a stone.

If she had cracked the code, she wouldn't have been able to sleep at night, but she slept. I lay awake and heard sounds of sleeping from the master bedroom. I would do what she had suggested, perhaps that was more important than me understanding her, there had been something about the way she had looked at me, besides, I, too, wanted to get rid of it. I fetched the cigar box from under my bed and put it in my PE bag along with a torch, a chisel and a pudding spoon I had smuggled from the kitchen, I put on a woolly jumper and woolly long johns and thick socks, I tiptoed to the window and opened it, cold wind against my face, there wasn't a sound to be heard and it wasn't as dark as last night because of the snow, I had done this many times. I climbed down the apple tree, then edged along the house wall in order not to leave any footprints, from the doorstep I jumped to the bushes bordering the fence to Mrs Benzen's, they had thorns which pricked, even in winter, but I was thickly dressed. I crawled to the secret hiding place where no one would find me, where the wire fencing between the gardens didn't reach all the way down to the ground, I dug a hole in the ground big enough for the cigar box, on Mrs Benzen's side just to be sure, I packed the earth I had dug up over and around it and scattered dirt and leaves on top for camouflage, I crawled back and returned the way I had come, I climbed up the apple tree, closed the window and went to bed, it felt as if I had rid myself of a great burden.

I drive into town, then put on warm clothes to go for a walk. It's eight-thirty, I'll get there at ten or just after and everyone will be in front of their TVs or getting ready for bed. I could wait until midnight, but that might be scary. I walk in the evening. It's dark, but the city centre is lit up, Christmas decorations sparkle and glitter, I walk through an area which is new and therefore not dangerous, through slush and slurry I walk, but I'm wearing sturdy boots, a thick coat, a beanie, mittens, glum-looking people rush by, weighed down by bags, I reach the historic part of the city centre, which has changed little architecturally, but the signs, the shops, the cafés are all new, the people who frequent them are dressed in grey, they stoop, they wait with faces which belong to a city bigger than the one I grew up in, there are more buses and they are longer, I walk on. The park is tranquil, the trees are the same, black and spiky, the park hasn't changed and everything starts to look familiar. Behind the park lies the school, fortunately it has been extended and I don't recognise it, the outdoor areas are smaller than I remember them, probably because childhood remembers them much bigger. I don't linger by the school although I'm tempted, I walk the school route home, past former workers' houses now occupied by students and modern young couples with children, Christmas stars hang in their windows. I follow the busy road which Mum wouldn't let us cross, I reach what was once a kiosk and is now a firm of consultants, I walk along the quiet streets where spacious houses sit in gardens surrounded by trees and bushes decorated with fairy lights, swings and rotary dryers, cars parked outside, everyone is at home, the light is on behind the windows, but I don't see anyone. I pass the house where Bente Bærdal lived, it doesn't say Bærdal on the post box, it doesn't say anything on it now, perhaps it never did, I walk slowly. It says Thoresen on the Thoresens' post box, I have to be very careful. Bror Thoresen might live in the small, newly built annex, while his children and their children live in the main house, Bror Thoresen has grown small, childhood expanded.

I follow the bend in the road, but don't look ahead, I stare down at the pavement as I used to in order not to step on the cracks, I would grip the shoulder straps on my satchel and I would think about . . . what, I mustn't try so hard. I make a detour up Godthåpsgate to what was once an ice rink, but which I discover has now been turned into a nursery school, I walk around it and see the house, still yellow, but the gable ends aren't white as they were back then but green now and the east-facing windows have been replaced with bigger ones, good for those who are on the inside as well as for those who are on the outside. I follow the path which crosses the ground diagonally, it's much shorter than it used to be, all distances have changed and the copse is no longer where it was and the tennis court has gone, I stop where the path stops and I cross the street of my childhood, seeing the street sign invokes a sinking feeling in me, but everything is asleep, the houses, the trees, the whole street is asleep. It's incredible to think that it was once so awake that it branded me with capital letters; it's sleeping now, but it could wake up at any time, that's the problem. The cast-iron gate rises towards me as does the garden which is smaller than I remember it, but the apple tree is so near the window, which was mine once, that it must still be easy to climb down it should anyone need to. Luckily the garage is the same, if the garage had been knocked down, it would have been difficult for me to get my bearings, had it been knocked down and rebuilt, I'd have run the risk of the new garage covering the spot I'm looking for, then again, Mrs Benzen wouldn't permit anyone to build on her land, but Mrs Benzen is dead, but not Mum, it seems.

Feeling numb, I walk past the house, which I once called mine, ours. The light is on in what was once our kitchen window, which is probably still a kitchen window, I imagine Mum by the cooker with a strand of spaghetti on a fork. There is a man inside who raises his head and glances at me as I walk by in the light from the street lamp, but he can't know who I am or what my business is, a random passer-by on her way to a house further up, a restless soul out for an evening walk, nevertheless the song of my childhood starts to play and I fear the man in the window like I used to fear Mrs Benzen when I was little and still fear her even though she is dead, your childhood fears never die. There is no light in Mrs Benzen's windows except for the small lamp above the front door, the house looks dilapidated and abandoned, and no car is parked outside the house which was once mine, ours. But Mrs Benzen's house looks sad, tired and uninhabited, so it's easier to start from Mrs Benzen's side. I open the garden gate and walk behind the bushes along the wooden fence that faces the road to get to the metal boundary fence, but realise I'll have to scale it in order to reach the spot. From where I'm standing I can see the hall window, the same old one with the stained glass which no one can see through, I climb the fence and land in the bushes which have prickly thorns even in winter, I'm on familiar territory. It's as quiet as the grave. I walk to the garage door near the cast-iron gate where the man in the kitchen can, in theory, see me, but there are no lights over the garage. The garage wall was eight paces long when I was a child. For my almost-sixty-year-old legs, it is five and a half steps, I walk along the garage wall until I rediscover the stride of the girl I once was and take seventeen of her steps, I turn right and force my way through the prickly bushes, I'm dressed for it. I reach the fence and clear a space for myself, I take out the polystyrene sheet and sit down, slip off my mittens and touch the ground with my hands, it's cold yet warm, dry yet moist, I hang my torch from a branch so it lights up the spot I have found by measuring, then I put on my mittens and start digging, I have a chisel and a metal ladle. How much soil do earthworms produce in one night, in one year, in fifty years, how deep will I have to go, I dig, I pull out roots, I cut roots with a pair of scissors, I don't encounter any stones, it's a good place to dig.

Did she live out the best years of her life, as the saying goes, in this house, in this garden? How young she must have been.

I have dug a deep hole. I pile up the soil behind me in small heaps, no light has come on in any of Mrs Benzen's windows, Mrs Benzen now sleeps in a bed or in the ground, I dig, not for dear life, but I live intensely while I dig in a smell of soil, of winter earth in December near the garage of my childhood as I trespass on the strict Mrs Benzen's land, be she dead or alive, I dig as if I'm vomiting up soil and purging myself, throwing the earth of my childhood over my shoulder, I dig while the world lies silent and the house in which I once lived lies dark and the houses where the Arnesens and the Bubergs lived lie dark, I dig up dark soil and the deeper I dig, the darker it is, and I want to get to the end of that darkness, but I breathe calmly because there is no rush now, I drink in the vast night as I dig with my mouth open, then the metal ladle makes a sound of metal against metal, I wake up from the darkness and it's as if a light has come on.

I put down the chisel and the ladle, take off my mittens and brush away the soil with my hands carefully like an archaeologist, it looks like the lid of a cigar box. I clean it with a vegetable brush, I brush the soil off the sides, I use the chisel to prise open the lid.

I put the cigar box inside a pillowcase and place it in my bag along with my tools, I leave through the garden gate, there are no lights on in any of the windows, I walk back to the nursery school, which was once an ice rink, and call a cab, which takes me home.

It's one-thirty in the morning when I let myself into my flat, the fjord is dark, I'm glad to be high up. I go to my work desk and switch on the lamp, I sit down with a strange feeling of reverence, I take the cigar box out of the pillowcase, again I have to ease off the lid. At the top is the drawing from that Sunday when Mum was ill, yellowed but intact and unexpectedly sharp, all of a sudden I'm overcome by emotion for both of us, the figure is huge, drawn right to the edges of the paper as if there isn't room for Mum and all her hair, but her face is lean and hungry and yearning, her arms long and paralysed. Mum had pointed at the drawing and said with a distorted face: That's you!

I thought I was drawing Mum, but I was drawing myself, I thought I was studying Mum, but I was studying myself, so had I ultimately not got close to Mum or Mum's world with my pencils but only my own? It wasn't an original observation, of course, but it suddenly felt concrete and claustrophobic, would I never be able to get close to other people? Underneath it were four of the robber drawings, inspired by princesses from stickers and fairy tale books, quite uninteresting, one of them had a speech bubble with symbols for swearwords like those used in Donald Duck comics, the coded language I had forgotten. Underneath it a diary where I had made only one entry on the first page, my younger self's handwriting unexpectedly assured: *Today Mum asked me why I keep clearing my throat when I do my homework. But I couldn't explain it to her. She got cross. When I went to bed, I thought about it. I think it's because the throat is between the head and the heart. And when I do my homework, I can't feel my heart. And then I lock my throat so that my heart can't get into my head. But if I tell Mum, she will say I'm being silly.* Mum must have read it one morning while I was at school, but it wasn't the worst that could happen, was it? Or perhaps it was because Mum's throat was also locked and so my diary had to be buried together with a yellow tin box of Partagas Club 10 that had belonged to my grandfather on Mum's side. I had forgotten or repressed or not dared to understand that. Grandad smoked Partagas Club 10 cigarillos on his occasional visits, which were rare because he was a drunk, Dad's word, because Grandad got drunk and had to be sent home in a taxi and every time Dad would swear that this was the last time and he would complain that the smell of Partagas Club 10 cigarillos lingered in the house long after Grandad had gone, and yet Grandad would come back the following year and I was just as scared of him then as I had been the year before and of the smell of Partagas Club 10 cigarillos which Dad disliked so strongly and Grandad's swimming eyes and Mum's disappointment because Grandad got just as drunk as he had last year and had to be sent home in a taxi, never again, Dad said, and that Grandad must have had something in his pocket, I thought he meant a pistol. Aunt Grethe told me about one time when Grandad was sent home in a taxi, it must have been at Christmas since she was there, that Grandad had been in the navy during the war and seen many bad things, that Grandad drank to cope with his baggage, she said, that it was because Grandad had been at sea during the war and Grannie had a lung condition that Mum was brought up by Uncle Håkon in Hamar. I hold the yellow Partagas Club 10 tin in my hand and realise that Mum, too, had a childhood.

The first song I ever heard was Mum crying by my cradle.

Inside the tin box are scraps of paper with symbols I hadn't been able to decipher as a child, still legible, I tip them out on the desk and count them, I turn sixteen fragments into a plane ticket to Yellowstone, Montana.

Mum had bought a one-way ticket to Yellowstone, Montana, why was she going there? Had Dad found the ticket and torn it up and Mum got sick and couldn't come skiing? Mum did the ironing. She must have smoothed over so many things during these years. There were many secrets in the yellow house, I sensed it, Mum sensed it, but we closed our eyes because we couldn't handle what we might see if we dared to look because if we saw it and gave voice to it, the bubble would burst, and we didn't know what would come pouring out, most likely it would be something that would ruin the wall-to-wall carpet and then someone would have to get down on their knees to clean it up, and that someone would be Mum.

I get up at seven o'clock, but I don't call her until nine. She doesn't pick up. I hide my caller ID, she doesn't pick up, she knows it's me. Perhaps I should write a letter? Dear Mum?

Old people are supposed to remember more clearly events that happened a long time ago than what they did yesterday. So is Mum today thinking more about her youth than about my departure thirty years ago? Mum spends most of her time sitting on her own by the kitchen table or in front of the television, do her thoughts journey to the yellow house and the life she lived there? But if she wasn't happy back then, which she probably wasn't, why would she want to recall those years? Perhaps things got better in time?

Dear Mum?

But perhaps it would be a mistake to bring up the plane ticket to Yellowstone, Montana, because now she is happy that she didn't leave. But then she can tell me that! Is that what I want to hear? No. Why do I want to talk to her? Because she hasn't told her story. I want to hear her story in her own words.

Dear Mum!

As you probably know, I'm back in the country and I would like to see you. Don't you think it would do us both good to talk? A conversation between us doesn't need to be exhaustive or deep, I'm not suggesting that we discuss the past or relive situations which are probably distressing and uncomfortable for both of us, but just tell each other a little about the life we live now? The other day I came across Grandad's cigarillo box, I think it was, and which you gave me once. It was a Sunday, you were ill and couldn't go skiing, and I was also ill and couldn't go skiing, we were home alone and I drew a picture of you and you gave me a yellow tin box that had Partagas Club 10 cigarillos on the lid, I think it must have been Grandad's? I remember it as a good day.

   Best wishes your daughter Johanna

At the bottom I wrote my phone number and address.

I was impatient and restless, I thought about driving to her flat, sneaking up to the green door at the back and slipping my letter into her post box, but if she found it without a stamp or postmark, she would realise that I had encroached on her territory and reject me. I drove to the nearest post office, which was in a shop, and posted it, they said it would probably be delivered the next day. Then I drove to the log cabin to calm down.

I didn't get a reply. My phone didn't ring, there were no beeps announcing a text message. No email. I spent five days in the cabin so that I could reasonably expect a reply in my post box when I returned to town; it was still empty.

Small private letters are sometimes lost in between all the junk mail. Mum isn't used to getting personal letters, she isn't expecting any letters other than bills in brown envelopes and so she chucks the contents of her post box straight into the recycling bin without checking if any small private letters might be hiding among the junk mail. I wrote her a text message: I sent you a letter, did you get it?

She didn't reply.

And why should she? I had banned myself from thinking about her, from contemplating or even acknowledging my feelings for her for decades, and now when I had a need to explore them, was I expecting her to be at my beck and call?

I had started to suspect that my image of her had frozen, that I had allocated her a special place in my mind, cast her in a role for which there was no foundation, and now I wanted to give her a more appropriate place, but how could I when she refused to talk to me?

But she doesn't give a toss about what kind of image you have of her and the role in which you have cast her in your narcissistic mind! Get over yourself! She couldn't care less!

I crave Mum's unfiltered flow of words, her stream of consciousness. How was it for you, Mum, tell me without fear, Mum, pour out your heart to me, Mum, why would she, of course she's not going to do that, she doesn't trust me, she might suspect that I have an agenda, that once we have met I will paint an unfavourable picture of her and exhibit it at the retrospective, but that's not how I work! But is that really what she thinks? She *must* have so many questions about me! About Mark! About John! Or she wants to rage at me for something! There must be something she wants to get off her chest given the many ways in which my presence in this world must have affected her life, she *must* want to share her opinion about so many things with me, but she is prevented from doing so by my sister who hates the thought that I take up so much space in Mum that Mum can't ever air her wish to talk to me, not even her desire to rage at me and so she has repressed it for years in order not to lose my sister as well and to please her to the extent that she has succeeded in burying it completely, am I dead to Mum?

Or do I blame my sister to make it easier for myself? I have female friends who are in regular contact with their aged mothers yet remain consumed by crucial questions, which they don't ask because they fear their mother's agitation, rage or rejection, nor do they believe that they would get a reply even if they did pluck up the courage to ask, and the few who did ask and weren't met with rage or rejection, got indifferent replies along the lines of: Well, who knows, life isn't easy, and so on. Why did Dad kill himself? Why didn't Aunt Erika and Uncle Geir ever speak, why aren't you in touch with your brother, why was Aunt Augusta not invited to the party? Well, who knows, life is hard. I yearn for something unobtainable. There's a real risk that I would leave a meeting with Mum no wiser than I am now or possibly more frustrated, a meeting where Mum and I just talked about the weather. But wouldn't that in itself be progress? No, I would probably leave a meeting with Mum where we just talked about the weather with a deeper, more paralysing sense of disappointment than the one I currently have, so why can't I just accept the situation as it is, my common sense already has, but pig-headedness makes me write to Mum, I don't understand myself. Up until now I believed I understood my problems, my grief, even when it was utterly paralysing, such as when Mark died, I could still recognise myself in it, but I no longer understand myself. Am I deliberately dragging out saying goodbye to Mum? She challenged me as a child and vanquished me as a child, as an adult I challenged and vanquished her, and is it spite or determination that now prevents me from leaving the battlefield?

I went to my studio as I always did when I was utterly confused, I grabbed a brush and painted the battlefield as it has been depicted for centuries, dead and mutilated soldiers, civilians pouncing on the dead and nearly dead to loot their weapons, water, jewellery, injured people trying to bandage themselves, when I put down my brush, I think, Am I exploring her childhood war trauma?

I have to talk to her about that!

When I rang her doorbell, she did open the door.

I don't think Mum was a happy child, I don't remember Mum telling us anything nice about her childhood. I don't think Mum was a happy teenager, I don't remember Mum telling us anything funny or positive from her youth. Mum was brought up by Uncle Håkon and Aunt Ågot in Hamar because her father was a drunk and her mother got lung disease and then died, perhaps Mum felt that Håkon and Ågot regarded her as a charity case, whatever it was she never talked about it. Håkon and Ågot never visited us, we would sometimes visit them before Christmas when November was at its worst, its coldest and greyest, we would buy half a disgusting pig from them and Dad would be desperate to get home, Dad hated visiting the smallholding which reminded him of where Mum had come from, Dad wanted to turn Mum into a Hauk. Away from the impoverished smallholding in Hamar, Mum could look like a movie star, her long copper hair, her porcelain white skin, her pale brown eyes, and Mum would rather be Dad's film star than live on charity in Hamar. Håkon and Ågot died unremarkably, the circle of life, I have a vague memory of Mum catching the train to Hamar to attend their funerals, perhaps my memory is wrong. Dad wanted Mum all to himself and Mum wanted to be Dad's because Dad was a fine man from a venerable family she should be grateful to be accepted into, Mum tried to be grateful, but the pain and grief of her childhood didn't go away just because she became Dad's, how would she cope with it? Mum couldn't cope with it, she couldn't cope with herself, but to whom could she pour out her heart? She never talked to anyone, not even herself. Relegated to domesticity, the kitchen and the darkness of the laundry basement, especially in the bleak November mornings, Mum felt her heart swell and fill with a confusing agitation after she had sent me to school and walked Ruth to nursery, Mum sitting at the kitchen table before she started her daily, dull, humiliating chores. I understand it little by little, but too late. Mum!

Or I use words to create my image of you.

I can't ring the bell at street level because then she will ask me over the intercom who I am and when she hears it's me, she won't let me in, she isn't allowed. I must ring the bell on the third floor, tomorrow, at ten-thirty after Ruth has called and asked her how she slept and if she has taken her medication, when she has had her breakfast and is sitting with her news-paper. December is a month of dark mornings, but also a month of shopping trips with Rigmor, so many Christmas presents to buy, but ten-thirty is too early for shopping, ten-thirty is the right time.

I take the car, find somewhere to park, pay for three hours just to be on the safe side. I mustn't hesitate, I mustn't think, just execute my plan. I enter the same way I did last time, but the green door is locked. I hadn't expected that, and I had just made myself emotionally ready. I look around, I can't see anyone, I hide in the cedars along the boundary fence where I have been before, I give it half an hour, vowing not to drift off as I did the last time, but stay alert. Ten minutes pass, everything is cocooned in silence, sparrows flutter around a bird table on the second floor, if Mum has a bird table on her balcony, she might be watching the sparrows there, I'm safe in the bushes and I don't hear any birdsong or cars, just my own determined breathing. The green door opens and the young man who came out to get his bicycle some weeks ago, a lifetime ago, leaves without locking the door behind him, he fetches his bicycle, which has winter tyres, and wheels it out, I go to the door, I open it and I enter, I would like to lock it, but I don't have a key. I don't take the lift, I walk up the stairs to the third floor, I stand in front of Mum's door and look at the nameplate. Like the other doors there is just a single name. The front door opens downstairs and I walk quietly up the stairs to the top floor, two men enter, they chat as they walk up the stairs to the first floor, it sounds as if they let themselves in, I walk down to Mum's door, there's no law against it, I just have to go for it, I ring the bell. I hear the sound of the bell inside, but no footsteps. With a kind of relief I wonder if she might not be home after all, yet I ring it again, I wait, I think I hear footsteps, I think I hear jingling, the door opens cautiously, she has the security chain on, behind it I see her face alarmed at the sight of me, it turns into a mask of horror, she retreats as if I were a monster, wild terror flits across her wide open eyes, she slams the door shut, Mum, I call out, I knock on the door, I just want to talk, I shout, that's all, I say, more calmly now, I knock on the door again but in vain, she has already called Ruth or the caretaker, I failed.

I walk calmly down the stairs and outside, the way you do when boundaries and taboos have been broken, I'm not quite so anxious now, I haven't broken the law, I go to my car, I get in, I take out my mobile, I send her a text: I didn't mean to frighten you. I just wanted to talk.

I notice that my hands are shaking.

There is no reply. I sit for a while waiting for one, but no.

I register that my heart is pounding, but not in the same old way, I'm angry now.

I drive to the cabin, it's a good decision.

It has snowed higher up, it's white. Mum's wide-open terrified eyes, I keep telling myself that I haven't done anything
wrong. My mobile is on silent at the bottom of my bag, I have
brought wine. I dust snow off the stone and sit on it, flat stones
are made for sitting on, I look at the glittering, untouched
whiteness around me, how infinitely beautiful it is and yet it's
not enough. Mum had been so far away that she couldn't see
me, she had placed a ghost where she imagined me to be and
she was terrified of it. I walk farther than ever because I have
never had a thought so heavy that I couldn't walk it off, so if I
just keep on walking, all will be well, as Kierkegaard writes, I
make a detour through the spruces where the forest floor is dark
and when I emerge, I see elk tracks across the mound and past
my windows, I let myself in and I am not alone in the world, I
light a fire in the brick fireplace and in the wood burner, I open
the wine, I pour a glass and I drink it, I don't take off my coat
until the thermometer shows the prescribed 18°C, it's in my
bones, dusk falls.

18°C, I take off my outdoor clothes and find my mobile, there is a text message from Ruth: *Don't you understand that Mum wants nothing to do with you. She doesn't want you to come to her door. She finds it rude and deeply distressing. She doesn't want any texts, letters or visits from you. If you don't respect this, there will be consequences.*

If I don't respect it, there will be consequences. What kind of consequences? Everything has consequences. The situation as it is now has consequences, that Ruth writes such a message has consequences. It is smouldering.

What bothers me is that she doesn't acknowledge in any way that the situation is difficult, that we are in a challenging existential dilemma. She writes as if they have never had any doubts, as if it has never been painful for them, she writes as if it's plain and simple and uncomplicated, as if they have acted on the basis of a rational, moral accounting: When Johanna does this, we react like that and we're perfectly entitled to do so.

But I know it's not true! Or at least it's not true of Mum, so why not admit it: the agony, the tears and the grief which aren't just about what the neighbours or other people might think, but about their relationship with me. But Ruth doesn't want to see or accept Mum's grief at our estrangement because it would make the situation more unmanageable for her, and yet the complexity is given away in the word *distressing* because if the situation had been plain and simple, the distress wouldn't be so great, the door wouldn't have been slammed shut so quickly, with such panic, there is pain there, admit it, and perhaps we could begin there?

Begin what?

What did you want her to have written?

That she thinks the situation is challenging, that she understands your wish for contact, but that she is in two minds.

236

Would it have made you feel any better if she had still said no, out of consideration for Mum?

Yes! And if she hadn't used the word rude! As if it were blindingly obvious that my humble request is inappropriate and unethical! And if she really believed that it's damaging to Mum's mental health that I write or call, then she could have written that Mum is going *out of her mind* and that would be an admission of culpability and responsibility. But she writes as if Mum has always done her best and if not everything has worked out well, it's down to chance or other people's mistakes, especially mine, so could I please suppress my egotistical urges rather than torment Mum with them, no, that's exactly what I can't! And besides, I can level the same charge at Ruth because she wants to keep Mum away from me purely for her own benefit, I'm quite sure of it, because I refuse to believe that deep down Mum wouldn't want to hear what I can tell her about my life, about Mark, especially about John, who has a son of his own, Erik, her great-grandson! If Mum is scared of responding to my approaches it's because she feels just as trapped now as she always has done, because her guardians had and still have all the power even if they acted and still act with the best intentions, tore up her plane ticket to Yellowstone, Montana, deleted my number on her phone, but someone who has her plane ticket torn to pieces or a number deleted from her phone, feels trapped and might end up hurting her fellow captives, her children say, because someone who has her plane ticket to Yellowstone, Montana torn to pieces and doesn't work and doesn't earn any money and doesn't drive a car and thus depends on someone who does, feels like a minor and is humiliated because it is humiliating to have one's life controlled and be treated like a child when you're an adult. And when that happens, you regress to childhood, like a recidivist criminal, a tough childhood that may have predestined you to end up in the arms of someone who will tear up your plane ticket and when that happens, you turn into the child you once were, the wound you received as a child and which you may have struggled to heal your whole life, is ripped open and you start to bleed again. You're in someone else's power, at someone else's mercy and that's why your heart is pounding, your brain seethes and if you can't cope with your pounding heart, your burning brain, but rage against life's limitations, the closed doors, the destroyer of the plane ticket and she who deletes a number on your mobile, by hitting your head against the wall, you're told that it's your mind that's twisted. I understand about the head, I also understand about the heart. A woman gives birth to a child and doesn't know how to care for the helpless creature placed in her arms that depends on her, on being cared for by her. But how do you care for it when you can't look after yourself? The child becomes a burden, the child becomes an impossible challenge, because how do you carry that burden, the child, when you can't carry the child you yourself were, the child that lives in all of us, especially in someone who lost her mother so young that she barely remembers her and thus carries her mother like a hole in her soul, like we all carry our mothers like a hole in our souls, small or big, living or dead, and so we all try to fill these voids so that we can live or we reject our mothers, but then – if we think we have succeeded – we have to live with the guilt of having rejected them. There is no freedom without guilt and, by the way, you were born guilty, you became guilty even as a child because of your family trauma and you passed on your pain to your sister or your doll which was damaged by being with you, trapped in a room in a house with a door too small to get out of, where every attempt would be a bloody, probably fatal, venture, but I blew up the door and it was bloody and now I'm here, in a cabin in the forest with an elk.

So I tell myself I have successfully rejected my mother, ha-ha!

When I was fourteen and had stopped eating, I would some-times argue politics with Mum, she always thought the same as Dad, but couldn't defend her views when he wasn't there, she thought I lacked respect when I contradicted her, she said, Have you no heart?

Another variation was: Your heart has become so hard.

And because she was my Mum, the hurtful things she said were always more hurtful than if someone else had said them.

At age fourteen I had forgotten the occasion when I'd made the diary entry about my heart and head and throat, and by then my diary had long been buried in Mrs Benzen's garden, there was great distance between the years back then. The diary and everything I had buried with it a long time before had been repressed out of great necessity. You are wiser at ten than you are at fourteen.

I thought a great deal about my hard heart because I could feel that it was hard and I wondered what it would be like to have a soft one, and I spoke to Pax about it, and he had read, he said, about someone who claimed that his mind was deep in his heart and said perhaps that applied to me too, and I wondered if by throwing up so much recently, I might have cleared the passage between my heart and my head so that they were now communicating and it was obviously a threat to my parents if my heart and brain started talking to each other while Mum's throat was still locked, and so she only ever consulted what she called her heart, which lied to her.

I wrote, Dear Ruth! I understand that Mum was unprepared when I called on her today. But I only did it because she hasn't replied to any of my polite approaches. I have no wish to torment Mum or start a conversation which would distress her in any way. But I believe that we have much to talk about, that Mum must have questions about my life and work which I can and would like to answer and vice versa. That is all I'm asking.

Best wishes, Johanna.

I sent it at eight thirty in the evening and hoped for a reply that same night, when it hadn't arrived by ten-thirty, I realised that I wouldn't get one.

Owls fly when dusk falls, the darkness grows denser and the wind shakes the forest. I turn off the light, go to bed and listen to the susurration from the swaying trees which increases in intensity, the wind is so brutal I think birds' nests must be torn from the branches and fall to the ground, that it's raining birds' nests. The trees groan and their far-reaching roots creak in the wild deep below my cabin, the earth quivers and my bed sails and the darkness grows darker, but not dark enough for the mystery which is too dense, too impenetrable, dark matter exists even if it can't be measured in any way, I can feel it in my body.

We all share the human condition. We are all lost in an existence with no obvious meaning or purpose; however hard we try,
we will never escape the uncertainty, the looming dangers,
illnesses that will come, the losses and griefs that await us, the
lost child, sibling, the past that suddenly comes back and knocks
on our door. We will all experience, we have all experienced,
someone we love and can't live without falling ill and dying and
all we can do is sit by their sick bed, their deathbed, powerless
and paralysed, and when the people we can't live without die,
then we must watch over them as they slowly grow colder and
paler, and afterwards we have to go out into noisy, busy streets,
flashing traffic lights, crows cawing in the trees, burdened by all
the practical tasks we need to deal with for the funeral and don't
forget to compose a death notice for the newspaper. We have all
experienced it and we will experience it again, and after the
funeral we mourn for weeks, years, perhaps right until we face
our own moment of annihilation. But if someone who has hurt
you dies, or someone you have hurt dies, before you have
resolved your relationship with them, because you have never
had an honest conversation, because the human condition was
never a subject for conversation, it will probably be worse and
add more stones to your burden than if you had had an honest
conversation, had tried to understand one another to the extent

that was possible, an illuminating conversation would most likely have lessened the pointlessness, the futility, our basic existential conditions, there is so little that is within our power, so little that is within our capacity, but this one thing is.

I live a secret life in Mum's mind and Mum lives a secret one in mine, but I'm in the process of unearthing her from the darkness, dragging her out into the light, and slowly she emerges because I want it to happen.

I remember a photograph, I guess it was taken when I turned eighteen or nineteen, no, it was when I started university, that's right, when I had been offered a place to read Law, that's right, so I must have been nineteen years and six months old. Mum and I are standing on the university's square, Dad took the picture, the university itself is in the background, I wore a purple dress, I think, now I don't know if I remember it because of the photograph which I pasted into the album where I kept official pictures, school photographs, confirmation photos, obviously, pictures from Christmas and birthdays and Constitution Day, photographs Dad gave me, Dad took the pictures. I threw away the album before I left with Mark, I remember packing clothes, toiletries, artist's materials, but nothing else, I owned nothing else, I left everything behind in Dad's flat, none of it belonged to me, the teapot, the towels, not even the books were mine, I held the album, I weighed it in my hands, then I went to the waste disposal chute and let it go.

The university in the background, Mum in a moss-green trouser suit fashionable in those days, slim, her loose hair held back by a dark blue Alice band, arm in arm with me, I'm pale with my not quite so abundant red hair in a plait to the side, very serious next to Mum, smiling at Dad, the photographer, but now I zoom in on us. I was nineteen years and six months old and I knew nothing, but I had started a tentative conversation with myself, I had started a discourse. Mum was over forty, her future was already determined and she knew it, but how would she react to the degree of insight and repression she was relegated to living in, did she give up on the conversation with herself? To live consciously is a great strain. Mum was cut off from her true feelings, and had adopted phrases, learned formulas and conventional gestures: A fool and his money are soon parted. It looks as if we are standing together on the university steps, but I had stopped caring about her moral considerations, her 'people don't do that', her decency arguments, my attention had been directed at her for years, I had wondered what she *wanted*, what she felt, deep in her heart, as they say, but at the university square I had given up finding out, when I zoom in on my own face I see a nineteen-year-old with a broken heart and the object of my grief is standing next to me in a trouser suit, and all these years later she fills me with compassion, poor Mum. But perhaps my memory plays tricks on me, perhaps I distort, falsify and misrepresent my memories in an attempt to understand myself now, do I reinvent them so that I can bear them, do I edit them so they don't challenge my current pain threshold? Do I fight an inner battle, conduct an inner dialogue with Mum, do I conduct ongoing negotiations about what happened and how and why and what was fair?

I woke up to this: You don't seem to understand the pain and grief you have caused your family with your grotesque pictures. You have never shown any kind of gratitude for everything Mum and Dad have given you and done for you for all those years, the countless gifts from Mum before you decided to just walk out on your husband and parents, on the contrary, you have caricatured them in deeply offensive ways in order to make yourself interesting, dress yourself up in your bad childhood because that's what an 'artist' is supposed to do. What do you think it was like for Mum and Dad when *Child and Mother* was exhibited at Gråtveit? Mum didn't leave the house for six months because she was so conscious of people's looks and gossip, and she had no way of defending herself. You have stolen Mum's life and presented to the world an account of Mum for which there is no foundation, but how are people supposed to know that, how you twist everything to make it fit your narrative without ever once considering that other people's narratives are equally valuable. And you didn't come home when Dad was ill, you didn't come back for Dad's funeral. If only you knew Mum's grief and shock at that. Right up until the church doors closed behind us, she was hoping that you would turn up and be with us at this very special moment, as a family. Mum thought about killing herself back then and I fear that she still might if you don't stop contacting her. You have displayed a callousness which is unforgivable. We both ask you to stay away. You have no right to anything, from Mum or from me.

She didn't sign her name. We are no longer on first name terms. Left *your husband and parents*, she wrote, she didn't mention herself, the sister, either because she didn't care or because there was no hint of a sister in any of my paintings.

The forest is whiter and quieter than yesterday, a muffling, calming blanket of snow has fallen during the second half of the night when the storm died down and I slept soundly, it's better to stay here.

It's true. I have no right to anything, all I can do is take on board that this is how they view the situation, my paintings, which they regard as an indirect, no, a direct criticism of the family, it would seem, but surely it's their problem that they interpret them so subjectively? Should an artist not be allowed to name her works with words such as child, mother, father, family, because her actual mother, father, family might view them as depictions of themselves?

Yes, of course, but be honest, didn't you have your own mother in mind when you made those works? No, it was the feeling of being a child I sought to express, a feeling I probably share with many people, but which is, of course, inextricably linked to the people at whose mercy that child is, I was trying to express the child's dependency, all children are dependent, it was dependency I wanted to express back when I was still struggling with it. Should I have refrained from exploring a complex parent-child relationship in which many will recognise themselves, because *one* specific mother might see herself in it and be hurt?

But an artist must accept that a specific mother might get hurt and be offended by a work of art, and not be surprised by it, especially when the mother in the painting has red hair, just like the artist's own mother. But I have red hair, I'm a mother, I had just become a mother when I painted the picture, perhaps that was why I painted it, it might just as easily have been a self-portrait because a painting always says more about its creator than about anyone else, don't they see that? Are they so myopic and self-obsessed that they only see themselves, and at the same time also believe that they have been portrayed incorrectly; it is us, but we're not like that! They fail to see the universal, they are so offended that it blinds them, they talk about *Mum's gifts* when what we ought to discuss is Mum's crises! From when I was very young I had an open wound and an open door over which I had no control, and Mum entered and infected me with her misery, and don't all children have that and don't all mothers do that, myself included?

Why are you protesting so vehemently? All they are asking is that you accept that the choice you made, back when you agreed to exhibit *Child and Mother 1* and *2* in their hometown, has had some consequences and you must learn to live with them.

No, I won't accept it, I can't accept it without objections and opposition and for reasons of principle, just as I will argue against anyone who clings to their hatred or is afraid to give up their hatred in order not to feel pain. I believe our estrangement fills Mum with despair, and if she doesn't feel despair, but only outrage and anger, then her outrage and anger merely mask her pain.

Mum has infected me with her inherited misery, have I in turn infected John with mine? But if I had, I would open up to him were he to indicate, in whatever way he chose, that I had, I would ask him to talk to me and try as hard as I could to see things from his point of view.

I call John, it's Sunday afternoon, he doesn't pick up.

We watched *Billy Elliot* together. John might have been sixteen. Mark hadn't died then, John had no sorrows that I knew of, but Mark was out, it was just John and me, we lay on separate sofas and we happened to be watching *Billy Elliot*, it was probably a Sunday. When young Billy read the letter from his late mother, a sound erupted from John, which he tried to stifle. I glanced towards him and saw a tear trickle from his left eye and I quickly averted my gaze, I realised that he was making no attempt to wipe it away so that I wouldn't notice it. What was it I mustn't see? Did he feel sorry for Billy who didn't have a mother he could talk to about his problems? Or did he identify with Billy even though he had me; did he not feel that he could talk to me about his problems, I didn't even know if he had any. But if Billy's mother had been alive, I told myself, there's no guarantee that he would have confided in her, as he told himself he would have done, because she was dead and it is easier to imagine a dead mother being good than a living one, and yet we imagine both the dead and the living mother as fundamentally good.

I look up *Child and Mother 1* and 2 on my laptop and everything I fled from comes back to me, the feeling of being a child,
but as form, the suffering comes back, but as form, that is art.

Art forms the artist, it disciplines her.

An artist doesn't address reality as such, only in the sense that it is artistically interesting. Real life is buying detergent and loo rolls, bus tickets, paying bills, cleaning your teeth, constipation, loading and unloading the dishwasher, real life is uninteresting, truth is interesting but hard to capture, homing in on it, pinpointing it.

The relationship of a work of art to reality is uninteresting, the work's relationship to the truth is crucial; the true value of the work doesn't lie in its relationship to a so-called reality, but in its effect on the observer.

Perhaps Mum sought professional help in the wake of *Child and Mother 1* and *2* in order to be able to cope with the psychological damage which I, according to Ruth, had inflicted on her. I have no wish to trivialise how that experience must have been, *Child and Mother* an unexpected message from the otherwise silent daughter across the sea, but it wasn't the worst that could happen, I'm guessing she had no illusions regarding my relationship with her, had I sent her *Child and Mother 1* and *2* privately, she would probably have been upset, but nothing more, it was the fact that it was on public display which tormented her the most. Even so I don't think she contacted a psychologist back then, to do so would be an admission of needing help with something other than practical tasks and Mum's issues were deep, the damage probably stemmed from her childhood. For that same reason she won't consider seeing a psychologist for support with processing the situation that has arisen now that the lost daughter is back and wants contact because a psychologist would ask her why she so adamantly and consistently rejects all approaches and what would she say to that?

She has put herself in a situation or been put in a situation where she can't articulate her grief at having lost a child.

I tell myself she prefers the company of people who tell her what she wants to hear, and that it's easy for them to tell Mum what she wants to hear because she probably comes across as fragile, because Mum was, or she was back when I knew her, an expert in putting on a sad and hurt face, the face of someone who has devoted herself to her trials and tribulations and made them her identity. In addition, she is old and we feel sorry for old people as a matter of course, they instinctively evoke our pity. The young hairdresser and the young doctor would show compassion were Mum to tell them how her older daughter had suddenly left the country and hadn't kept in touch for years, and now she has unexpectedly come back and is *demanding* something, and they probably won't wonder and they certainly won't be openly critical of Mum's version of events, the truth doesn't matter when you are faced with such a painful confession, and besides, what is the truth? If an old woman with a sad face and a trembling voice tells you about sad events in her life, you don't ask critical questions or invite a philosophical conversation about the distribution of guilt, you don't turn into Gregers Werle, your instinct is to console.

I'm ashamed that such an ordinary woman has such power over me, but then I remind myself that she pushed my body out of hers and put me, at her own initiative or when told to do so by others, to her breast, to which I latched on with my tiny jaw and drank vital fluid, and I probably experienced even at that early stage a fear that she might take revenge on my greed by consuming her own creation, then that didn't happen, instead I became the bearer of the pain she had succeeded in repressing.

Ruth doesn't mention Yellowstone, Montana. Mum has told her about my various approaches, but has she shown her the letter where I write about Yellowstone, Montana? Mum keeps Yellowstone, Montana hidden from Ruth, she presents her with a sleek narrative where nothing grates.

There were christening pictures. They came back to me with the morning coffee while I looked across the untouched white blanket outside, black and white. One of Dad's family in front of the stone church and one of just Mum and me, Mum holding me, the baby to be christened, up to her cheek, Mum's cheek against mine and we look happy, but surely it must have resounded in Mum on that occasion that not long after she herself was christened she was fostered by Uncle Håkon and Aunt Ågot in Hamar who already had a child to look after. Mum stands with her cheek against mine in front of the stone church and she looks happy, but what is Mum thinking? Perhaps there are christening pictures of my maternal grandmother with her cheek against Mum in front of a church somewhere, but if there are I have never seen them, and no one ever spoke about my maternal grandmother and rarely about Uncle Håkon and Aunt Ågot in Hamar because they were nothing to boast about.

As a child I studied her intensely, I watched her every move, I tried to read her and sense her longing, she was out of my reach. When I grew older, I approached her with a different, a linguistic curiosity, and at first she reacted with incomprehension, then by distancing herself, but worst of all: with stock phrases. As she opened her mouth, she turned me into a lonely and alienated child. A young woman had died in an avalanche in Rondane at Easter and I couldn't stop thinking about it, talking about it. Mum: But she shouldn't have walked so far. Quit while you're ahead. That's what I always say: People don't know what's good for them. At times I would observe her in company and wonder if perhaps I might like to have her as an aunt, a colleague or a friend, but as a mother she was no good for me, she inflicted emotional damage on me. Mothers smother. And yet I still hope for a calm and illuminating conversation with her, where does that hope come from? From my childhood?

The worst moments between us always happened when one or both of us were desperate, cornered. But if we were to meet in a neutral place, might that make us feel safe or would that place instantly become charged the moment we entered it?

The allegorical figure of justice, Justitia, is a woman. Because mothers are female and we entertain the idea that a mother loves all her children equally and would never treat them differently or show favouritism; a mother has the ability to dispense justice.

That's wishful thinking. A mother treats each child differently because she responds to her children's requests and the children don't approach her in the same way. I assume it's easier for a mother to like and be with the child who, as it grows older, continues to treat her with devotion, reverence or admiration, who doesn't look at the mother with a critical or accusatory gaze, but with one of understanding, and as the mother gazes mildly at the devoted child and frowns at the critical one, the battle begins. Siblings vie for their mother's love from an early age and the mother senses the children's fight for her, irrespective of whether the mother is good, capable or incapable, they fight over her, especially when the children are young, they fight a bloody battle for their mother, the family is the battlefield, the mother the queen, and the mother, who isn't a queen in any setting other than the domestic one, enjoys her queenly status and drags it out. Perhaps the battle is bloodier or more brutal if the mother is less capable, so the children have to fight harder for the little favour she does have to offer, and many mothers enjoy the battle and the blind

267

devotion it generates in a few of her offspring and feeds on the expressions of their need for her warmth and attention and tells herself they are evidence of her skill as a mother and as a human being, and so she strives, consciously or unconsciously, to stimulate the battle and prolong it, and the children aren't aware of it, they just want more of their mother like Ruth, once I was back in the country, I tell myself, wanted more of Mum than before, has won Mum and wants to keep what she has won and not share. I invent Ruth, that's what's so frightening, and Ruth invents me, and we both invent Mum.

I mustn't forget that there are many kinds of love and that people's love objects change throughout their life. An old man gets a new girlfriend and forgets the wife he lived with for forty years. I saw it when I had a summer job at a residential care home, how a few of the old residents were fonder of their care workers than of their adult children. When Mrs Ås's son had been to visit, she was disappointed that he had brought flowers when she had wanted chocolates, or vice versa, and disappointed that his wife hadn't come with him or that she had, and in any case, her son should never have married that woman and their children weren't worth much, either. But Mrs Ås loved Nina, her care worker. She never talked about her son apart from vilifying him the moment he left, but she spoke constantly about Nina in terms of endearment, asked about Nina when she wasn't on duty and would light up when she was. Whenever Mrs Ås rang her bell and I responded, I knew she would ask for Nina and wait for her no matter how long if Nina was at work. And Grannie Margrethe, too, must have bonded with her care workers at the private care home where she spent her final years, I remember her funeral. It was while I was starving myself and the cakes at the wake were tempting, but I resisted and I remember how Dad reacted when a care worker from her home gave a eulogy and referred to his mother by her first name, Margrethe. She talked about how Margrethe would come to the nursing station when she couldn't sleep at night and what a nice time they had had, playing cards and swapping stories because Margrethe enjoyed talking about her life, she said, while Dad bit his lip. And Margrethe would cheat at poker, said the carer in her broad local accent and winked, and Dad cringed at the end of the table and gestured to the toastmaster to cut the woman off, I recognised that gesture, but the toastmaster didn't do as he was told and the carer got to paint a picture of Margrethe Hauk that was utterly alien to me, and probably also to Dad, judging by the look on his face. True, I hadn't met her very often, but I remembered her voice from telephone calls on my birthday, deep, terse, authoritarian, while the carer spoke as if Margrethe had been easy-going, charming and open, and Dad looked peevish and didn't stop talking about how appalling it was that some fat, ill-educated woman had claimed that Mrs Margrethe Hauk had cheated at cards, for seven hours as we drove home from Bergen.

All children depend on their mother for their survival and will, as a result, be forever vulnerable to her, body and soul; for that reason we have ambivalent feelings towards mothers and that's why mothers are often absent in feel-good films. The maternal figure, warts and all, triggers emotions far too complex for feel-good. In the feel-good movie beyond all other feel-good movies, *Love Actually*, mothers are absent or they exist as peripheral, supporting characters, despite the many other love and family relationships the film otherwise explores. Of the mothers featured, the most central one is dead, another less a mother and more an about-to-be-deceived wife, and she is presumably an about-to-be-deceived wife because she is a mother to such an extent that she is incapable of leaving her unfaithful husband. The movie would have been ruined if mothers had occupied the place they have in real life, with all their complexity, I write as a mother. There is no mother in *Hedda Gabler*, while General Gabler and his pistols loom large, Jørgen Tesman's blessed father Jochum is dead, we are told, but his mother is never mentioned; when a mother is a central character in any of Ibsen's plays, she is often what we back then, and still, would call a bad mother. In the mighty works of Søren Kierkegaard, his epistles, letters and diaries included, where the father recurs as the root of the son's torments and his psyche, his faith and his writing, the mother isn't mentioned once, not with a single word.

271

The mother in real life, our experience of the individual, actual mother, is interwoven with the mythical mother, poor Mum and every mother and I who all bear the mythological cross.

I had tried to imagine how I would react if John had suddenly left and moved far away without warning. I would have taken it badly, I would have asked myself what I had done wrong. Not because he had left and certainly not if he had done so to follow a woman with whom he was in love or to pursue an education which was only available where he was going, no, I don't think so, but I would have asked myself why he hadn't talked to me first. Because I wouldn't have tried to talk him out of it or criticised his decision, I would have supported him as indeed I had done when he told me that he and Ann were moving to Denmark, I'm quite sure of it. But I couldn't talk to Mum and Dad about my plans because they would have become hysterical, told me they wouldn't allow it, they might even have tried to prevent me physically, locked me up, I don't think I'm making this up. I contemplated telling them I was leaving, but then decided against it because I was afraid that Dad would contact Mark and threaten him or kill him, I felt physically sick with fear, but perhaps these scenarios were merely the product of my strong sense of guilt because I knew how hard my leaving would hit my parents socially. Thorleif never even crossed my mind, isn't that strange, or perhaps it isn't now that I understand much more than I did back then. John had moved far away, but not out of the blue, and he had discussed the move with me and from the very first moment I had said: Go! Perhaps I said so too eagerly? I added that I liked Ann and I was pleased that they had both found work in Copenhagen and I never mentioned that I knew there were vacancies in the Los Angeles Philharmonic, should I have done that?

I tell myself that if he were to write me a letter to address complex issues in his relationship with me, I would say that I understood, I tell myself a lot of strange things.

Snatch the blindfold from your eyes, paint your eyes open, paint their eyes open, it's in your power!

I go to my studio to the dizzying smell of paint and turpentine and dip my brush in the white tin, then I stand in front of the canvas, my arms limp, the brush dripping paint onto the floor, I count the drops and get to six.

I try to recall buried images of Mum, but it's as if those few photographs I remember from the discarded album take up all the space, and I need to get beyond it, behind them.

It's essential to me to be connected to the boundless and the infinite. And I can only experience that connection when I'm aware of my narrow limitations, the experience of being both finite and eternal, me and the other, Mum. Only when I experience being *just* me, little me, do I sense the boundless infinity, and only by being conscious of it can I avoid becoming the victim of my subconscious. If I remain ignorant of anything that intrudes from my subconscious, I risk becoming at one with it. Man's task, Jung writes, is to develop consciousness.

It's about crossing the threshold to a hidden world which exists in this world, the invisible transition between what we understand and what we can't understand, the experience of crossing a border, it's the return of memories we have repressed that changes the landscape, the crucial jigsaw piece you sensed was missing turns up, the picture presents differently and you have to reacquaint yourself with the new in something that is old, it's like sewing a button on a stuffed cushion, the needle goes through the seat of the chair and when the sewing cotton is tightened, the cushion starts to take shape.

The subject is too big, it might well give me a nervous break-down.

I had dealt with the practicalities of real life, loo rolls and washing-up liquid and could return to the white forest. I retraced my own footsteps, I had created a path, a wound, it deepened as I walked, I felt the pain gather in my chest and in my left forearm, was I keeping the wound open and making it deeper?

I could smell powder snow and the air was cold against my face like the time I came home early from school, I must have been nine because we had been taught by the new maths teacher, Hagås, so I would have been in Year Three, I worked out. Hagås walked from desk to desk and asked if we understood the questions, I understood them, and that's how it all got started. I finished first and walked home alone through empty streets covered in powder snow, the air cold against my face like now and a memory comes back which I didn't know that I had forgotten, I came home and surprised Mum. I opened the front door and she called out, startled, from behind another door: Who is that? in a fearful voice, but it couldn't have been anyone but me. Ruth was at nursery, Ruth didn't walk home on her own and Dad was at work, it had to be me. And yet Mum was frightened when she heard the front door open and I called out: Only me! It made no difference, I could smell fear, I heard her lock the bathroom door again, she was in the bathroom, but that wasn't the problem, was it?

I, too, grew scared now, Mum's fear triggering mine, but maybe she had just gone to the loo where everyone wants privacy, I quickly took off my coat and walked upstairs with my heart pounding, I saw the locked bathroom door, I went to my room and sat on the bed with the door ajar, it felt like a long time before Mum emerged without having flushed the loo, she was wearing her dressing gown over her skirt and tights, the cord around her waist tied tight, it looked weird, she went to the master bedroom without looking at me and emerged after a short time without the dressing gown, but in the same blue checked skirt and now wearing a long-sleeved grey jumper, and she went to the kitchen. I sneaked out and over to the kitchen door to watch her, she was standing by the cooker with her back to me, I had come home too early for Mum and I decided to go back out and meet up with a friend. I went to the bathroom to have a pee before I left and I noticed a bowl in the bath tub where a white blouse with rust coloured stains near the cuff of one sleeve was soaking, she knocked on the door almost immediately, she shook the handle, ordered me to unlock it, I did as I was told, she tore open the door, rushed over the bath tub, I said I needed to pee, she replied that I could do that while she was there, she tipped the brownish water out of the bowl and turned on the bath tap, put the bowl underneath the running, clear water, she stood with her back to me, but with her hands in the bowl, rubbing the soiled garment with frantic hands, I watched her elbows move up and down, I suddenly didn't need to pee after all and left the bathroom hesitantly. Stained clothes must be soaked overnight and then rinsed out three times, I went to my room, but I didn't close the door. Mum came out after having rinsed out her blouse more than three times, the sleeves of her jumper were wet because she hadn't pushed them up and now, in the cabin, the realisation hits me as clear as the running water, but deeper and redder, Mum the fire from Hamar, Mum the blood from Hamar.

Mum always wore long-sleeved blouses, dresses and jumpers, also in the summer, Mum never went swimming, she never wore a swimming costume or a bikini. Mum had fine white stripes on her left forearm, I saw them when she bathed Ruth and I sat on the lavatory lid, watching them, I was sometimes allowed to do that, I thought it was something she was born with, one of nature's variations, a genetic decoration like her red hair, like her freckles that looked like the dusting of chocolate on a cappuccino, thin white stripes like a piece of finely woven linen on her forearm when she thought I wasn't looking, never in the kitchen or in the living room, never outside, not even in the garden in the summer, all Mum's blouses, all Mum's dresses had long sleeves, but until this moment I hadn't understood why, what could have caused the white lines, not until now.

Mum in the kitchen staring emptily out of the window at the terrible light that appears on certain autumn days in November when it is very cold, the kind of cold that blows through your body even if you are indoors, a chlorine yellow and ochre light reminiscent of dried blood, which stains the sky that lies heavily over the houses and the ice rink, which makes marks on the tarmac look like dogs that have been run over, which turns dirt in puddles on the road into poisonous reptiles about to rise up and cross the road and crawl into the house to sting and bite, Mum consumed by a wordless darkness, the future mute and dark, Mum's throat tightens, Mum's chest aches from being locked up, her pain has no way out, Mum's chest constricted by the cold and the reptiles crawl across the road and Mum's breath is trapped inside her and with no one to turn to, Mum goes to the bathroom, she takes one of Dad's thin razor blades and frees her breath.

I'm reminded of a little bird I found in the forest in the spring, it lay flapping a broken wing, incapable of moving from the spot where it had happened to land.

Scars don't disappear, the scars on Mum's left forearm must still be there, I need to see Mum's left forearm as proof.

I call Mum, she doesn't pick up, she has made up her mind. I text: Dear Mum! There is so much I want to talk to you about! I think it could do us both good!

Best wishes your daughter Johanna

There is no reply.

Mum must have been desperate, but more importantly lonely and ashamed. What if someone had found out that she went to the bathroom and eased her pain with a razor blade? Dad didn't see it, Dad didn't want to see it and didn't understand or didn't take an interest in anything other than business and Mum's tumbling copper hair. Later Mum found another way of solving the problem of her pain, was that lucky for her and unlucky for me? Mum encapsulated her mental anguish and adopted society's conventions in every area of her life, its rules and principles, she internalised them as a map, which she followed without ever wavering and she never questioned it, it was a safe map from which to navigate, it provided unequivocal answers to every question, every dilemma, it never failed, she was on safe ground as long as she consulted it, but in order for it to be as valid as she needed it to be, it also had to apply to everyone else, especially her daughters, for whom she drew the map and then shoved it down our throats and forced us to swallow it, she rammed the map into our ears with her talk of dos and don'ts, wash your hands before you eat, have you remembered to say thank you, a constant unstoppable stream as if the meaningless noise that erupted from her mouth could muffle the torment of her heart, as if she could exorcise her demons with her wittering and she tried to draw sustenance from the young daughters in her proximity, and she ruled over them by controlling and dominating them as compensation for her own dependence, blocking them from anything that might lessen her influence, me in particular, because she could feel that I was distancing myself from her and I didn't show her *respect*, I was intrusive and invasive because the truth was she was powerless and I had stopped caring about her opinions about this and that, and I always had to draw attention to myself, asserting myself in ways she never could when Dad was present, she would enter my room when I had friends over to tell pointless stories about something she had done right, about someone who had complimented her on her ability to make sacrifices, Mum would enter my room and instantly hold court. The recurring narrative was: I have lived for others. She believed in the grandeur of her sacrifices or she had to believe in it. She would appear to have given up having her own dreams fulfilled and had consequently long since buried them, but they reappeared in a distorted form, as sudden outbursts of rage, especially when I attempted to pursue my own dreams; if you want to overcome self-denial and self-loathing, you must turn your shame into anger, but Mum directed her anger at me and my attempts at separation, and the rage that could have changed her world became impotent.

I have never had an honest conversation with her. Though we were both so talkative in our separate ways, we never had an honest conversation. Once I had a sense of kinship with her, but it was dishonest and it has long since disintegrated. It's the person she was when she was still in contact with her pain who interests me, that's the person I'm working on freeing myself from, a work which presumably can never end; I have to see Mum's left forearm.

I probably made a clumsy attempt as a child, but it was already too late. As an adult I tried on at least two occasions, the first was some months after I had travelled across the sea, I wrote a long letter to explain myself, it was as honest and open as I could make it, but I understood from the brief reply that the social scandal my leaving my marriage and my family had caused had hit her harder than the loss of me, and consequently my motives didn't interest her. I tried again not long after Dad's funeral when I had received the reproachful text message from Ruth about how badly, almost fatally, Mum had taken my absence, I wrote Mum a letter about my difficult personal circumstances, how Mark was seriously ill and John was only fifteen, but where I also very delicately intimated that Dad must have been a difficult man to live with, a strict patriarch who enforced his will in everything no matter what, controlled his surroundings through fear, she protested vociferously. Dad had been the best husband a woman could have, the best father a child could have, I ought to be grateful that Dad had been the father he was, he was beyond reproach, how dare I speak ill and with such lack of respect of the dead. Obviously I shouldn't allow myself to be hurt that Mum, who was wrong about most things, didn't understand me, and yet I was hurt. Yet again I received a painful illustration of how she closed her eyes to every uncomfortable truth and I gave up.

But was I now harbouring a fresh hope of talking to her? When the likelihood was that a woman of eighty years plus would defend her life choices tooth and nail rather than regret them and express her regret, that Mum would obstinately insist that following Dad's orders in everything, adopting Dad's recipe for life and his inherited system of norms without questioning them had been in her own best interests and especially in the interests of her daughters, it was more likely that Mum had long since stopped reflecting on the past, to explore, carpe diem and so on.

And yet I refused to believe it, I told myself she had remained a stranger to herself all her life and that she harboured a wish to be set free and I thought I could help her?

It was terribly naive.

But Mum had wept in the church.

It's said that old people experience a second childhood, but perhaps what they do is walk slowly back towards their childhood and so if Mum lives to be ninety, which she probably will, she might return to the point when she was alone in the bathroom and liberated her breath with a razor blade?

I get up in the darkness, I light a fire in the wood burner and in the brick fireplace, I make coffee and I drink it, I'm unable to eat anything, in the darkness I retrace my tracks to the car. Dawn arrives slowly as I drive towards the city, the sun grows mighty. Sunday 14 December, I hope Mum is going to church.

I park outside Arne Bruns gate 22, the church bells haven't started chiming yet, I turn off the engine, I'm warmly dressed, and yet I soon feel cold despite the 2°C outside and the sunshine, I restart the engine, having grown careless or indifferent, possibly defiant. The street is deserted, but why are the trees standing guard, Mum's apartment block lies quiet, but why does it look like a fortress? The church bells start to toll, but no one comes out, a snowplough appears and I have to move the car and turn around in the next junction, I follow the snowplough and park where I just was except with the car facing the other way, no one has yet emerged from Arne Bruns gate 22, I didn't lose sight of the entrance for more than a few seconds, the bells have stopped ringing, the service has started, and Mum isn't going. Perhaps Mum isn't in, perhaps Mum has gone away, perhaps Mum is celebrating Christmas in the Mediterranean, it's a terrible thought now that I'm so close. I turn off the engine and get out of the car, I cross the street and walk around the apartment block until I stand underneath Mum's balcony, luckily the light is on in Mum's windows, I stand on the snow-covered lawn and stare at them brazenly, there's no law against it, I bend down, scoop up a handful of snow and compress it into a ball, I throw it and I hit what I assume to be Mum's living room window, there are potted plants on the windowsill and a seven-armed candlestick, because of Christmas I assume, I haven't forgotten my old snowball-throwing skills, I wait, nothing happens. I bend down, scoop up another handful of snow, squeeze it into a ball, raise my arm, take aim, I throw it and bull's eye, it makes a louder noise than the first one, my throw was more powerful, I wait for Mum's shadow to appear behind the flowers, the scene resembles an old-fashioned proposal, maybe she will open the window and say yes. I can't see anything, I can't hear anything, I bend down, I scoop up a third handful of snow, I squeeze it into a hard ball and I throw it; just as I have let go of it I notice a shadow behind the flowers, the snowball hits the window which breaks, I run, that wasn't what I wanted to happen.

Ruth texted that they had reported the broken window to the police, but I never heard from the police, I'm guessing it was an empty threat; after all they couldn't be sure who had thrown the snowball. Yet still I didn't back down – or perhaps that was why I didn't – instead I came up with a plan.

At the same time I asked myself: What do you really want?

Knowledge!

Why? Because if I can confirm that Mum's left forearm is covered in fine white scars like loosely woven linen, then she can't deny her pain and even if she refuses to open up to me, I will, if I see those scars, gain a better understanding how she felt, the woman who cared for me when I was a child, whose pain must have poured from her heart and into mine. If I can understand her better, then perhaps I can forgive her!

But she doesn't think she has done anything that needs to be forgiven, regardless of the scars.

Is there a mother on earth who doesn't think she has done her child any harm, who doesn't need forgiveness? Yes, this mother, this particular mother, my mother because she has demonised her older child, she decided together with her younger child that everything that has been and is wrong with the family is the fault of the older child and that's why *it* has to ask for forgiveness! And perhaps I can, if I get to see her scars that is, cry belatedly over them and apologise that I understood her pain too late, how confused and trapped she must have felt.

But she doesn't give a toss about whether or not you understand, she has erased you to such an extent that she doesn't give a damn about your inner life and she definitely has no wish to rake over the past. She has survived through her strong ability to gloss over anything unpleasant and if something has helped you survive, you are loath to let it go, so forget all about it.

But the past isn't dead, it's not even the past! That's where Ibsen's characters run into trouble, thinking they can put the past behind them, yet it turns out repeatedly it doesn't work like that! So Mum will definitely be haunted by the past at some point or involuntarily at night, Yellowstone, Montana and all the dreams she had to give up because Dad's dreams always took precedence over hers. She thinks she has forgotten them, but they are inside her somewhere, as is the hole I left, a tiny little empty room where I once lived, no, Ruth has filled that space, and it's easier to carry Ruth inside her than me, I was a burden right from the start. So forget it! But that's exactly what I can't do! I can't forget Mum because I suspect that her early ambiguous love for me and her current obstinate refusal to engage with me reflect her own unresolved conflicts, and I want to know more about them. Mum's mystery is my mystery, it's the enigma of my life, and it feels as if it's only by getting closer to it that I can reach some kind of existential resolution.

But what if the challenge is to reconcile yourself with the unresolved?

Mum has suffered greatly because of her older child, I should write, I wrote that Mum had suffered greatly because of her older child.

Mum would laugh when I mimicked Mrs Benzen walking to the shops with her grannie trolley and shaking her fist at the cars coming towards her. Mum would laugh when I mimicked Miss Bye who would rock from side to side as she said grace with her eyes closed before we were allowed to open our packed lunches. When Dad wasn't present, Mum would laugh when I mimicked Grannie Margrethe's deep voice when she rang on my birthday: Johanna Hauk? I congratulate you on your birthday. I have sent you a fortune in the post.

From time to time Mum would say: What does Grannie Margrethe say when she calls on your birthday, and I would deepen my voice, put on a Bergen accent like Grannie Margrethe's and Mum would laugh, they were good times, Mum misses them.

Marguerite Duras writes somewhere that every mother in every childhood represents madness. That your mother is and always will be the strangest person you will ever meet, I think she's right. Many people will say when talking about their mothers: My Mum was mad, no, I mean it, mad. When we remember our mothers, we laugh a great deal, and it's funny.

I drive to the forest and I walk through fresh snow in the old tracks to the cabin and dream that night that Mum is sitting in the church, crying, and when the service is over and everyone has left, Mum stays in the pew just like I did, and the verger comes over and asks if she wants to talk to the vicar, and Mum nods and the verger fetches the vicar who bends down to Mum, and Mum says with her tearstained face and in a voice so childish that it breaks my heart, I'm so unhappy, I'm so lonely.

I wake up bathed in sweat and I understand that our earlier relationship has survived in me, that my former dependency on her, which I simultaneously treasured and detested, still lives in me.

I called her childish, I regret that, that was childish.

They take precautions after the broken window and I have to lie low. Mum doesn't go out on her own, she barricades herself in her flat and doesn't open the door when someone rings the bell, if someone rings the intercom she always asks who it is before letting them in. Ruth picks her up and drives her if there is anything she needs to do in town. My chances of bumping into Mum on her own are minimal.

I go to the cabin and I spend a week in solitude there, I draw Mum's features with charcoal. I don't care about the retrospective anymore. The elk appears without its antlers, the circle of life, its pelt has lightened, it's December, soon it will be Christmas. I leave them alone, they hope I have given up and drop their guard. They will want to light a candle on Dad's grave the day before Christmas Eve, this coming Saturday.

I draw Mum. She is swimming on her own. Dad fishes her out of the sea and drops her into a goldfish bowl. Mum is alone in the goldfish bowl, she knows that she isn't a goldfish and is scared of what Dad will do once he finds out. Mum is always scared. Mum gives birth to a daughter in the bowl, she isn't a goldfish, either, Dad discovers it immediately, why should he feed this strange, non-decorative creature, goldfish food is expensive. Mum tries to defend her offspring, *that's what I've been saying all along,* but it's too difficult, and the offspring takes off and jumps out of the bowl, fortunately the sea is close by, she lands in it and swims far away. Mum tries her best to look like a goldfish and makes a reasonable job of it, then Dad dies.

How was it for Mum when *Child and Mother 1* and *2* were exhibited at Gråtveit? Shameful and humiliating. How she must have wanted to scream: *You have no idea what it was like for me.* But she couldn't, it was impossible given where she was, she had to suppress her scream. Then Dad died, then I didn't come back for the funeral and Mum thought of me as lost and so she experienced a double loss, worse than the grief I experienced when Mark died, unbearable perhaps, and that insight has never crossed my mind until this moment.

In Rembrandt's painting *The Return of the Prodigal Son*, the younger son kneels humbly in front of his aged, grey-bearded father as he begs for forgiveness for leaving him, he understands he is no longer worthy to be his son, but asks instead to be his servant. The father places his hands on his son's shoulders, they radiate unconditional love and his face beams with deep paternal joy, the irreplaceable child he had lost has been given back to him.

It's beautiful, but it doesn't belong to the human sphere. Rembrandt's father represents God and shows us how God welcomes all lost sinners, the greatness of God's mercy. But if our earthly father and earthly mother were anything like God, there would have been no need for us to invent Him.

So there's nothing that painting can teach you?
    What would that be?
    To be humble, to yield.

If I could meet her without being frightened or doubting, not proud of my success or vengeful, but completely humble and trusting, with the greatest devotion, and see Mum through the eyes of a child, a gaze that entrusts my entire destiny to her, the noise of the traffic would still, the rustling of the trees would cease, we would be surrounded by total silence and she would be unable to resist.

Having the courage to do that.

I recall the sight of the elk that one time I thought it had gone mad, when it scared me, in order to summon up the courage to do it. I could tell the moment it arrived that it had a purpose, what was it? Its antlers were bigger than ever, so heavy that I thought they must be difficult to carry. It didn't amble along with its usual sedate dignity, it was restless as if it was in pain or going out of its mind as it followed its familiar path across the mound towards the cabin and I waited for it to continue on its usual route when it turned abruptly, lowered its head and charged at the copse of dwarf birches less than two metres from the cabin wall, it smashed straight into them without reducing its speed, desperate or furious or crazy, bashing its antlers against the branches, sweeping them over the birches, rubbing the tines up and down the tree trunks and the shrub as if it had got caught in it and was trying to tear itself free or entangle itself further in a snare, as if it was trying to trap itself, its mighty rear body shaking in its attempt to get the unmanageable antlers and the many tines to come to their senses, it crashed into the branches over and over, sweeping its head from side to side until bloodstained strips hung from the antlers and over its eyes and nose, yet it carried on butting, it took off and rammed its antlers into the mesh of branches again and again and it looked like an act of frustrated self-harm and self-destruction or a protest against the existential condition on earth, it carried on for so long that it began to exhaust itself and I feared it would collapse, pass out, it looked like a fatally wounded animal. But then the last bloody strips of velvet fell from the antlers and landed on the ground or were left hanging from the birch branches like strange fruit or bizarre Christmas decorations, and suddenly its antlers were shiny and bone-white with a marble sheen, finally freed from their shell, their skin, their protective husk, ready at last to defend its world against the outside world.

I drive back to the flat the day before I'm going to do it. The city is decorated for Christmas, but the snow has melted and turned into grimy slush. There are queues of cars at the entrances to the big shopping centres on the outskirts of the city even at two o'clock that Friday afternoon. Cars spit out exhaust fumes while the people inside them are tormented by all the things they have to buy. Impatience quivers in the polluted air. Around three o'clock I enter my studio and hang up the charcoal drawings, the elk with and without its velvet, with and without its antlers, I long to go back to its habitat, but I have a job to do. Pax has called, but I can't talk to him either, I don't want good advice.

I sleep fitfully and I wake up hot, having set the radiators at too high a temperature last night. I get up and open the door to the balcony, I need the cold air against my face and hands, and I know: Today's the day.

I dress up warm, layers of thermal underwear and over them my snowsuit from the ice-sculpture trip to Alaska, I sit on a chair on the balcony drinking coffee with warm milk as a ship leaves the port with a string of flashing red Christmas lights along the gunwales, the hooting from the funnel suits the mood, it's almost time. I'm unable to eat anything, I drive to Arne Bruns gate, I park the car, it's a quarter past eleven. I see no one, I get out and cross the street to the maple tree in the garden behind the apartment block that is number 24, I stand close to the thick trunk with my face turned towards the yew tree hedge along the fence, listening intensely, but hearing only a hollow whooshing from the big road some blocks away. I'm calm and composed. It's a doddle. I have been there for less than fifteen minutes when I hear the sound of a car, I go to the hedge and part the branches, Ruth's red Volvo parks right behind my car. Ruth gets out dressed as when I last saw her in a dark all-weather jacket with a dark grey scarf around her neck, short light grey hair, which stands up, steamed up glasses, a hiking rucksack on her back, I wasn't wrong.

Twenty minutes later they appear, walking arm in arm down the pavement right past me, Mum closer to me, I think I can hear her breathe and smell her smell, but perhaps it's all in my mind, she wears an olive-green all-weather jacket, grey scarf around her neck, the green bobble hat on her head, they both wear dark trousers and thick boots as if they had bought them in the same place, together. They walk in step, they sway in step, they have swayed in step for so long that they have forgotten it's what they do, they are numb, they are dumb, they believe their own narrative, or perhaps it's all in my mind.

I follow them to the cemetery, I know the way and I don't have to follow them closely, once they reach Dad's grave, they stop, obviously, Ruth sets down her rucksack, takes out a blue polystyrene sheet and kneels down, clears away the old wreath and brushes aside pine needles and wet leaves, Mum stands like she did the last time with her legs slightly apart and her hands folded tightly behind her back. They don't say anything, I sit silently behind the bushes, listening. A woman comes walking in my direction with a dog on a leash, which wants to say hello to me because I look like a dog, crouching behind the bushes, it sniffs me, I hope its owner won't ask me why I am squatting on my haunches, listening in the silence, I place a finger across my lips, she looks at me quizzically, but she says nothing and carries on walking, she spots Ruth and Mum, then looks at me again, I smile so that she will think this is a game. The dog refuses to move on, its owner calls it, Fido, of all things, my sister turns her head, but doesn't see me. The dog obeys its owner, as you would expect. Ruth finds a new wreath in her rucksack and places it where the old one was, removes the burned-out grave light, finds a new one in her rucksack, lights it and sets it down behind the wreath, which is round with red berries, listen how quiet it is. Then she stands up and goes to dispose of the withered wreath and the burned out grave candle in the rubbish bin close to me, returns the polystyrene sheet to her rucksack and stands next to Mum, I watch them from the back, alike yet not alike, Mum with a certain decisiveness in her legs, Ruth with a bend in her knees like a bird, as if Mum is the boss even though she is the dependent one now, Mum's power is great, Mum's power is great. Mum starts moving, one foot in front of the other, Ruth follows like a shadow, they walk around the tree behind grave like the last time, it's not raining now, I'm not crying now, I follow them at a safe distance, Mum has been waiting for Ruth, she takes Ruth's arm, they sway behind graves and trees, snow falls and melts on the withered grass and the earth, and then the tarmac, we won't get a white Christmas this year, but I will go to the cabin, possibly even tomorrow. They pass Ruth's car, will she walk Mum all the way up to her flat this time? Ruth escorts Mum, holds Mum's arm, and Mum sinks into Ruth's arm as if she were a victim, she would like to be a victim, she thinks it suits her, I feel a rage rise in me. They stop at the entrance to Arne Bruns gate 22, Ruth gives Mum a hug, turns and walks back to her car, I stop behind the birch, Ruth gets into the red car, Mum stays where she is, watching her, she opens her bag to take out her keys, I expect, she finds her keys, Ruth starts the car, pulls out and drives past Mum, who puts on a sad face, waves a lonely wave with the keys in her hand, but Ruth can't live with Mum. Ruth's car disappears, Mum turns towards to door and walks up to it, I walk carefully up to the point where she was standing just now and follow behind her, she won't turn around, her hearing isn't what it was, she is focused on the keys in her hand and is aiming at the keyhole, finds it, unlocks the door and gives it a soft push, it's one of those doors which will slowly open itself, a door for old people, Mum enters without looking back, the door starts to close slowly, Mum passes the post boxes, I have plenty of time,

322

Mum has reached the lift, I place my left foot between the door and the frame, I lean against the brick wall, if Mum turns now, she won't see me, but she doesn't, the lift arrives, Mum enters, the lift doors slide shut, I slip inside and run up the stairs past the third floor, I get there before her, here comes the lift. Mum gets out, I sneak down, she has her keys ready in her hand, she unlocks the door, enters, the door starts to close behind her, I put my left foot on the threshold and push the door open with my hand, Mum turns, sees me and her heart stops, she screams, but I'm already inside.

I stand with my back to the door, she retreats to what would appear to be the living room, she has recovered and says: Get out!

I say: Mum!

She says: How dare you! Get out!

I say: I just want to talk.

She says: I've said all I want to say to you!

I say: Five minutes, that's all I'm asking, I only need five minutes, there are things I would like to know, things that are very important to me, she repeats: Get out!

I say: Mum!

She narrows her eyes as if the sight of me disgusts her: I'll call my neighbour! I'll scream if you don't leave. I'll call the police! Get out!

I say: Am I that easy to write off?

She says: You created this situation, this is your fault, those terrible pictures of yours!

It wasn't you! Mum!

Oh! What do you think people think!

Why do you care what people think?

Don't give me that! As if you're better than the rest of us! You've always acted as if you're better than the rest of us, but you're not, far from it! You're not well, everyone says so, you're not well!

I recognise that pitch from my youth, her tone of voice and

324

those words from my youth, her rigid stance, her defiance and anger from my youth and the paralysis of my own youth, my throat choking with tears and just like I did back then I slump down and all I want to do is run because my onerous self-reflection work feels utterly in vain. And yet I don't leave because suffering is a link which brings a magical pleasure happiness can never deliver. Or because we might learn something when we are in the middle of it?

I say: So you're not to blame?

Mum: Don't you start talking about blame! Get out, I say, I'm calling the police!

I say: Call the police! Tell me about Yellowstone, Montana! Get out!

I know you cut yourself with Dad's razor blades when I was little!

Her face distorts, her mouth curls down, her brows narrow, I recognise that mouth, that face, the strained, grim face of repression, puckered eyes glowering with bitterness and hatred, but also the black fear at the bottom of the very same eyes, Mum!

You're lying! You're a liar! All you ever do is lie!

Then show me your arms!

Get out, she repeats, get out, she is screaming now, deviating from the rules for good behaviour she has stuck to and been suppressed by her entire life, it would be liberating if I wasn't on the receiving end of it and I, too, wasn't terrified.

So you're scared to show me my left forearm? Show me your left arm, I say, I demand, at last I feel the rage surge in me. Get out, she screams. Show me your arm and I'll leave, I say, to my surprise I hear that my voice is trembling.

Go, Mum shouts, get out of my house, Mum hisses, her

voice oozing hatred and I finally understand: She wants me dead. She finds her mobile in her bag, moves further back into what must be her living room, I'm calling the police, she shouts, I follow her, I raise my arm to knock the phone out of her hand, but I don't dare, she presses three keys, emergency services would be my guess, I knock the phone out of her hand, it hits the floor, I get to it first, I'm faster, I hurl it at the wall, it hits a picture which smashes, she turns to it, now she is more scared than aggressive, that's progress, I realise she thinks I'm going to kill her, she thinks I hate her as much as she hates me and am capable of killing, you judge others as yourself. She flings her handbag at me, I swat it out of the way before it hits me, it lands on the floor, she screams louder now so all the neighbours must be able to hear, time is running out and this is my last chance, I grab her jacket, she screams, I pull the jacket off her by tearing at her left sleeve, she falls to the floor, I bend over her and push back the sleeve of her jumper and I see the scars, white scars of suffering, the proof that I'm not mad. I knew it, I say, I knew it, I say, I let her go, I straighten up and I look at her, I knew it, I say, she lies on the floor with her right hand clutching her left forearm as if to hide it, her right hand has automatically found her left arm, poor Mum, but what can I do, Mum is mute, Mum is paralysed, I have paralysed Mum, she thinks I'm going to kill her, that is how she looks, as if her last moment has come, as if she has already been killed by her daughter, I have killed her, I shake my head. You won't have to see me again, I say, I shake my head, it happens spontaneously, I shake my head, I open the door, you won't have to see me ever again, I say and I mean it, I really don't want to see her again, it's enough now.

I step out into the hallway, I turn and I look at her one last time, her eyes are wide open, You're a terrible human being, she says, I close the door, she calls out: I wish I'd never given birth to you. You're not who you think you are, she says.

I walk down the stairs and I leave.

How I love my Mum in the bathroom with the razor blade, the desperate Mum of my past.

I drive to the cabin through fog and sleet, the windscreen wipers can't handle the water that sheets down from the open, grey sky, I drive as if in a trance, buzzing with electricity.

I wish I'd never given birth to you. You're not who you think you are.

I had tried to understand her from a distance for a long time, but had come to the conclusion that I couldn't, that my images of her were frozen and static, and I realised that I had to see her in person, then she didn't want to see me, and then I sought her out in an attempt to understand who she was now, only to learn that the frozen images were true, that the softer images my reflections over the last year had produced didn't match any kind of reality. She quite simply didn't care what I was thinking.

She had abdicated her role as my mother, I was dead to her. She had succeeded.

Meanwhile I had set her aside, put her on ice, and had convinced myself that it was within my power to defrost her when I was ready. I had failed.

I arrive, I walk the path through the forest, I reach the cabin and let myself in. It's not until I sit down that the paralysing pain of my childhood comes back, I had expected it, but not like that. I had thought the pain was familiar to me, that it had faded and become manageable, but it envelops me with renewed vigour. Fortunately experience has taught me that when it hurts so much I think I'll pass out, that's when it starts to evaporate. Like people who lose a limb in an accident say they didn't feel a thing because the nervous system can't transmit that much pain to the brain, the system is overloaded, that's what will happen if I let it come without fighting it.

I had made manifest something which was previously invisible and disproved something which had previously seemed likely, which was that she must love me somehow.

Yet her rejection hit me harder than I had expected, it felt as if she would never stop abandoning me.

I had to abandon all hope, shed my antlers which had been so heavy to carry, I had to meet all of my own needs.

There are many ways to leave your mother, more than fifty. I put on my Sunday best, I get myself into a solemn state of mind and go to my place of high expectations, the graveyard of disappointed hopes, the big forest. I have brought the cigar box and the blue gingham bed linen, the yellow bird, I carry them all and grow heavy as I do so, I regain the lost weight of my childhood as I carry Mum on my back as I have carried her with me always, a heavy burden, Mum will leave a scar on my shoulder, it's not until now that I realise how deep that wound is as I carry Mum far into the big forest where the spruces stand so close that there is no snow and the ground doesn't freeze, where it is possible to hear the murmuring of the dead among the trees. I find a suitable spot in between a living anthill and a rotting tree stump, I dig a hole in the ground with a chisel and a metal ladle, I unpack Mum and I study her one final time, she at whose breast I nestled, in whose arms I lay as a child, safe and warm, perhaps, her whose safe haven I sought when I was scared, whose lap I curled up on when I was sad, she who I would ask, Hide me, Mum, but who didn't have anywhere to hide herself, no place of refuge, I drank impossibility from Mum, the pain ran from her breast into my mouth and out into the rest of my body, but something in me understood it and resisted and from that moment I tried to get away from her impossibility and pain. I have travelled widely, Mum, but probably walked in circles most of the time, Mum, carrying you and your heavy sadness, Mum, but it has to end now, Mum, I'm tired, Mum, and I have nothing more to say, Mum, I'm going to my shelter, Mum, I was a child once with dreams of finding you and now I'm a woman and I give you up, I say goodbye and I bury you, I lift you from me and set you down and cover you with moss and mulch, I remember the smell of your jacket as I pulled it off you and of your jumper when I pushed up the sleeve, I don't like that smell anymore, it's a sign. Earth to earth, ashes to ashes, dust to dust, then I leave without looking back.

I terminate both rental agreements and pack up my things, I go home to where I do my best work, Utah, it is finished.

Mum is dead in me, yet still she stirs from time to time.

Three things remain: Clothes must be soaked overnight and then rinsed out three times. Spaghetti is cooked when it sticks to the tiled splashback behind the cooker. A fool and his money are soon parted.

The most important one is the one about the spaghetti.